The Big I Am

by

Robert Farquhar

First published in Great Britain in 2020
by SNB Publishing Limited. 57, Orrell Lane,
Liverpool L9 8BX

NO PERFORMANCE MAY BE GIVEN WITHOUT A LICENCE

Productions

All enquiries regarding production rights should be
addressed to :

The Knight Hall Agency
Lower Ground floor
No 7 Mallow Street
London EC1Y 8RQ
Tel 020 3397 2901
email office@knighthallagency.com

The Big I Am was first performed at the Everyman Theatre, Liverpool - 16 June to 14 July 2018

Original cast

Helen, Feral Boy, Elizabeth, Barmaid, Ensemble	**Nadia Anim**
Vera, Ruby, Ensemble	**Emma Bispham**
Peer Gynt 3, King, Fred, Ensemble	**Richard Bremmer**
Priest, Ensemble	**Patrick Brennan**
Bridegroom, Bob, Vicar, Ensemble	**George Caple**
Dad, Ronnie, Elvis, Rag & Bone Man,Ensemble	**Paul Duckworth**
Main Hippie, Compere, Ensemble	**Marc Elliott**
Geezer Vicar, Strange Passenger, Rag & Bone Assistant,Ensemble	**Cerith Flinn**
Cynthia, Doreen, Nurse, Air Stewardess,Ensemble	**Emily Hughes**
Peer Gynt 1, Ensemble	**Nathan McMullen**
Sylvie, Maureen, Divine, Ensemble	**Zelina Rebeiro**
Mother, Green Woman, Ensemble	**Golda Rosheuvel**
Ma, Gustav, Ensemble	**Keddy Sutton**
Peer Gynt 2, Father, Ensemble	**Liam Tobin**

Director	**Nick Bagnall**
Designers	**Molly Lacey Davies**
	Jocelyn Meall
Composer	**James Fortune**
Musical Supervisor	**George Francis**
Lighting Designer	**Kay Haynes**
Sound Design	**Everyman Sound Department**
Movement & Fight Director	**Kev McCurdy**
Assistant Designer	**Natalie Johnson**
Assistant Director	**Jack Cooper**
AV Coordinator	**Jamie Jenkin**
Casting Director	**Sophie Parrott CDG**
Artistic Director	**Gemma Bodinetz**
Executive Director	**Deborah Aydon**

For
PHYLLIS FARQUHAR
(1926 - 2016)

ACT ONE

Darkness. A low rumble. Builds. Then. The shadows and sounds of fighter planes. A blitzkrieg. This is World War 2. The north of England. It is 1941 or thereabouts. A bomb falling. Explosion. Then.

A woman in the throes of giving birth. Some neighbours helping. Doctor arrives. Noise drowns everything. A man stands at a distance, observing. He has a suitcase. He turns to leave. The woman giving birth lurches forward. Shouts out.

She is MA. He is DAD.

MA Hey. You. Where do you think you're buggering off?

No answer.

MA Here's me giving birth in the middle of a flaming bomb rattle, and there's you. Eh? Scuttling off, saying sweet effing nowt.

No answer.

MA Do you hear me? I said -

DAD Yes Ma. I heard you. Even though I'm somewhere else waiting for a train. I still heard you.

MA Go on then. Sling your hook.

He starts to leave.

MA But, eh. Just in case you're thinking. I'm not going be coming out with any of that last minute, oh, poor me, please stay, why don't you? Oh no. None of that. Not even on my death bed Mister. And I won't be mouthing, I miss you neither. Not even when I'm sat up, in the middle of the dark, drowning in heartbreak. I won't say it. And nor will he. Even though he'll probably want to. Because he's a lad. And lads need Dads don't they? Lads need Dads like they need a hole through the heart.

DAD Are you finished?

MA Yea. I'm finished.

DAD starts to move away.

MA And good bloody riddance. You, you rubbish, cheating husband, you.

DAD stops.

DAD Alright yea. I do. I feel guilty. And I will think about him. Now and then. But, I can't -

MA Are you still here?

DAD I can't be doing with any of this.

MA Eff off you bastard!

DAD And anyway. I've already got a family in Scarborough.

The whistle of a bomb falling.

DAD You won't see me again.

Explosion. Shift back to MA giving birth. The baby is born. MA holds him close. The scene disperses. The baby is passed on. Eventually it is thrown through the air. It is caught by PEER GYNT. Full of youth and arrogance. He looks at it.

PG And to think that was me.

Throws the baby off stage. MA appears.
It is now 1961 or thereabouts.

MA Hey you. You Peer Gynt.

PG Alright Ma.

PG attempts to explain himself. MA won't let him get a word in.

MA Where the blazing bloody hell's, bloody, teeth, have you been all this, bloody time? Five whole days, five whole nights, you've not been here. No word, nothing. Just me, and that empty back bedroom, with all of them filthy, dirty, dirty, filthy pictures of nudie women stuck about all over it, and -

PG Look Ma. Will you. Just give us a minute. I can explain. If you could, just. Ma, if you could let me explain myself.

PG drinks from a milk bottle.

MA Oi. Don't do that. Common as dog dirt that is.

PG Alright. Keep your hairnet on.

MA I've been worried sick I have.

PG Well, take your tablets then.

Again PG tries to make his case, whilst MA holds forth.

MA Take your tablets, he says. What use are tablets to me, when it's me heart, and me nervous system, that you, you bugger, carry on ransacking.

PG Here we go. Eh Ma. Eh? Can I? Can I get a word in?

MA Go on then.

PG Right. God's honest this is.

MA Liar!

PG What?

MA All the lies you tell. I'm surprised you still know your own name.

PG Look. I was in town.

MA Were you now?

PG I was. I was in town. And I was -

MA Drinking. Drinking till you dropped down, dead pissed, in the middle of the street.

PG And who said that?

MA Is what I heard.

PG Alright. Yea. I had a drink. And a few more on top of that. But, listen, right. I swear, on my life -

MA To lie. To lie, drink, fight, and fornicate. Have that on your tombstone.

PG Do you know what? I'm not staying here if –

PG again tries to make himself heard.

MA Go on then. First sign anything gets in the way of all them whoppers you spout, and he's off. Just like him. Eh. Him the two-timing, two-faced, toe-rag, who shall never, ever be mentioned, in this house -

PG Because what's the point? If you just kick off every time. Don't mention him then.

MA Do you hear me?

PG Alright Ma. Alright. I do drink. I do fight. And I do-

MA Fornicate.

PG But that doesn't mean -

MA Doesn't mean what?

PG It doesn't mean, I don't still love you, does it?

MA And now he says that. You're a right crafty bugger you.

PG And five nights ago this was.

MA What was?

PG This was. This. What I'm about to tell. As I stumbled out of the pub, full of big thoughts, and dark ale.

MA Sounds about right.

PG And sat there. In the lamplight. Lit like it was in a film or something.

MA Was what?

PG Was this dog Ma. All brown, and floppy ears.

MA Oh. A dog you say?

PG And, I'm telling you now, it had the saddest eyes.

MA I love dogs.

PG I know you do Ma.

MA And I love dogs with sad eyes.

PG I know you do.

MA I would loved to have had a dog.

PG And that dog would have loved to have had a Ma. I thought that very thought.

MA You're not too bad a lad really, are you?

PG But then. Just as I stepped towards.

MA What?

PG This fellar. There he was. Lurching up out of the shadows. And you could smell it on him. A right, nasty bastard. And then before I knew it. His fingers and thumbs, they were tight round its throat. And, oh, Ma, the noise that dog made. It would have broke your heart.

MA It is breaking my heart.

PG And so I thought. No. Not on fellar.

MA Go on Peer Gynt.

PG And I was over there. And I grabbed him. Just like he had hold of -

MA Geronimo!

PG Eh?

MA I've always wanted a dog called Geronimo.

PG Alright Ma. Yea. Just like he had hold of Geronimo. And then -

MA Did you thump him Peer Gynt?

PG I did Ma.

MA Well done lad.

PG I thumped him till he was out cold, and going nowhere.

MA Good boy.

PG But Ma. But. Whilst all this was going on.

MA What?

PG He legged it. Geronimo was gone.

MA Eh, but do you know what? I would have done the same.

PG So what I did -

MA Even though I've got a bad chest, and a funny hip.

PG I took chase.

MA Well done son. After him.

PG I took flight. His tail fast dissolving. And I'll tell you now Ma, there was no way he was going be making off now. No way. Not now I wanted him for you. Hey you. I shouted.

MA Geronimo!

PG Geronimo! Come back here now. That's what I said. That's what I roared.

MA Even though you didn't know -

PG No, but -

MA He was actually going to be called Geronimo.

PG No, but I wasn't thinking about that. Because. There we were. In full pelt. Him, and me. Adrenalin sky high. The moonlight bouncing off us.

MA Go on Peer Gynt.

PG But then Ma. But then.

MA Oh no. Not another but then.

PG I whistled round this corner. And.

MA Where was he?

PG My very thoughts. But. There. Just as. Just as I was about to give up hope. There he was. In the shadow. Skulking, and smirking. But before I could make a move, he reeled back, eyes glinting, heart in his legs, and he was off. And I was off after as well. But this time Ma, it began to dawn. As there we went. Cobbles. Street lights. Hard stone underfoot. What became clear. This, now, this chase was not that, it was a game. We were like a couple of stir-mad crazy lads grabbing life, and running wild with it. The front room lights of a thousand indifferent lives flying by. And then there's a wall, and we're up it, and over it. And then. A washing line. And a shed. And some dustbins. They go spinning. And then. There's a drainpipe. And we're up it. Easy as. And there we are. The city stretched out, off, over there somewhere. And we're now, look at us, we're dancing tiptoe along a rooftop precipice. Like blood mates. Like soul chums. Unleashed. With all this unbridled fizz. Alive with the sheer electric shock of existence. But then. There's a rush, and a push, and we're off, over the edge, and now. We're in the air. Entwined in it we are, as we break into weightlessness. And tumble, like sky-skimming, slow-motion, wingless birds of prey. Swinging in the breeze breath. Oh yea Ma. There we go. We fall. We slow-dive. Down, and down. Until.

Holds the moment.

MA What? What next? What then?

PG As luck would have it.

MA What?

PG As we're about to hit the ground. And break into a thousand tiny bits.

MA Say it.

PG A lorry came past.

MA Eh?

PG And there's a mattress in the back.

MA A what?

PG And we soft land. And -

MA Hold on. You mean to say? A lorry? With a mattress? Just happened to be passing -

PG I know Ma.

MA At that very moment?

PG And it was then, that Geronimo, he turned to me. And he said. Well, I must say Peer Gynt, that was a piece of luck.

MA Oh! You?

PG is laughing. MA is raging.

MA You bloody great big bloody liar! Come here. Oh. You told a load of made-up rubbish, and I just sat here, believing every, single, flaming word of it.

MA is now up and after him round the table.

PG I spun a story Ma. I thought you liked stories.

MA A talking, flaming, dog. And all that running about. Over rooftops and what have you. Come here. You cheeky rascal bastard. And, eh. You're not too big for a slap across the arse you.

MA, out-of-breath, sits back down.

MA You'll be the death of me you will.

PG No Ma. I won't be the death of you. Life. That's what'll be the death of you.

MA Always the smart arse. You'll come to no more than sweet effing nothing you.

PG Yea, but you love me really.

MA Love you? I spawned you. I've got no choice in the matter

PG And anyway. I will be a big someone, something one day.

MA Just a load of old guff.

PG Scoff on Ma. But you'll see. Because. Look at it round here. Everyone's so dead scared to even dare do anything out of the everyday. It's all just flat caps, and twitching curtains, and, oh, eh, mustn't grumble, and God Save the bloody Queen. And I'm not going along with any of that. I'm not having it.

MA If I've heard it once.

PG I'm going be a King I am. I'm going be an Emperor.

MA Are you now?

PG You'll wake up one day, and I'll be gone missing, adventure wanted.

MA And how are you going do all that then? Eh? Because the last time I looked, that piggy bank of yours, it was full of nothing but a handful of halfpennies.

PG I'll be alright Jack.

MA You should have married, oh, what's her name? When you had the chance.

PG Who?

MA You know. Her? Her with the Dad. The Dad with all the cash.

PG Ma? Who -

MA Because look at the state of us. Threadbare don't even begin to cover it.

PG Who are you talking about?

MA What's her name?

PG Belinda?

MA No.

PG Priscilla?

MA No.

PG Maureen?

MA No.

PG Doreen?

MA No!

PG Princess bloody Margaret?

MA Hey. Now, don't you take the piss Peer Gynt-

PG Cynthia?

MA Yes!

PG Of course. Cynthia!

MA That's the one. Her Dad, now, he is proper self-made minted.

PG And do you know what Ma?

MA You'd have been feet under the table, well in there lad.

PG I'm going go now, and look her out.

MA I don't think so. Not today you're not.

PG Why not?

MA I'll tell you why not. Because she's getting married.

This stops PG.

PG She's what? When?

MA Today. Sometime, ooh, about now.

PG Who to?

MA Micky. Er? What's his name.

PG Micky? That fish-faced, virgin sap. Why is she marrying him?

MA Too late to ask her now. You'll just have to stay in with me, and -

PG Sorry Ma, but I don't think so.

MA Hey. Where do you think you're going?

PG I just said didn't I? I'm off to see Cynthia.

MA is standing in his way.

MA No Peer Gynt. It's the girl's wedding day. The last thing she needs is you turning up, and creating merry ding-dong.

PG Out of my way Ma.

MA Let's stay in. Listen to the wireless.

PG Ma! Will you? Get out the way.

MA No. I want you to stay here, and not do -

PG Ma! Please. Will you just -

MA I forbid you now. Do you hear me?

PG Hey Ma. Now. Here's an idea. Why don't you come with me?

MA Behave yourself.

PG And we can dance the night away. What do you say? Have some fun for once.

MA No. I'm too old to be having fun. Now you listen to me, and do as you're told for once.

PG Alright Ma. Alright. Only one thing for it.

PG picks up MA.

MA Hey. What are you doing now? Stop that. Peer Gynt! Put me down.

PG Sorry Ma. It's for the best. In you go.

PG puts her in a cupboard. Shuts the door on her.

MA Hell's bells. The cheek of it. Peer Gynt! Let me out of here now.

PG I'll see you later Ma.

MA Go on then. Suit yourself.

PG I will Ma. I will. Because. What else is there? Eh? What else is there?

MA bangs on the door. PG exits, laughing. Music crashes in. The scene shifts. A working-class northern English wedding. An early sixties combo. The stage fills up. Glad rags. Lots of drink.

A BRIDE (CYNTHIA), in emotional distress, rushes across the stage. She is pursued by FATHER and MOTHER. This scene is happening away from the main body of the wedding.

FATHER Cynthia! Will you get back here. Cynthia!

MOTHER Oi you, you mardy little madam. Come back here now.

FATHER Cynthia!

CYNTHIA What?

FATHER What do you think you're playing at?

MOTHER Good question Father. Answer him. Go on.

FATHER Do you hear me?

MOTHER Running off like this. At her own wedding. Who does she think she is?

FATHER Good point, well made Mother.

MOTHER Thank you Father.

FATHER I'm speaking to you Cynthia. Did she hear me Mother?

CYNTHIA Of course I flaming well heard you. I haven't just suddenly gone deaf have I?

FATHER Right then. Well maybe you -

MOTHER And don't speak to your Father like that.

FATHER Thank you Mother.

MOTHER Thank you Father.

FATHER And don't speak to your Mother like that as well, whilst we're on the subject.

CYNTHIA Oh Christ! You two. You're ridiculous.

MOTHER I knew the day you were born, you were trouble.

CYNTHIA Why don't you ever listen to me? I never wanted any of this.

CYNTHIA starts throwing bits of her wedding paraphernalia at them.

FATHER Oh. Eh. Well, now. I'll tell you what young lady, it's far too late, long gone in the day, for you to be, eh, to be saying that now. Because do you. Eh? Are you listening? Do you know how much I've dished out for all this, whatsit, this palaver? The flowers. The cars. The food. The booze. The fellar taking all the snapshots. Not to say nothing about all the fancy do-dahs, and what-nots.

MOTHER Because fancy do-dahs, and what-nots do not grow on trees do they?

FATHER No, they don't. Well said Mother.

MOTHER Thank you Father.

CYNTHIA Will you, just, listen to yourselves. The pair of you. You're a joke. Like this whole sorry, fucking charade.

FATHER Oh. Oh. I don't believe what I've just heard.

MOTHER Wash your mouth out.

FATHER She just said the F word Mother.

MOTHER You filthy-tongued bitch.

CYNTHIA Leave me alone!

She runs off. They follow on.

FATHER Hey you. Hey! Come back here now.

MOTHER I'm not having this. Not on my big day I'm not.

FATHER I put a lot of effort into that speech just now. Do you think she heard me Mother?

MOTHER She heard you Father.

They have gone. PG appears. Drink in hand. The stage is suddenly full of clouds. Eerily beautiful.

PG Oh now. Look. Up there. Look. The clouds. All mad and fluffed up. Always there. And no one ever sees it, and thinks. How bewildered and always strange it all is. And look. Now. There. It's me. It's Peer Gynt. Free-spinning, and swimming in all of it.

Two female GUESTS pass by.

GUEST(F1) Listen to him.

GUEST(F2) Always going on about himself.

GUEST(F1) Right odd one he is.

GUEST(F2) Oi Peer Gynt. You're strange in the head you are.

They exit. Laughing.

PG Hey! You, and your prattle. Because what's it like to be so, deadly empty dead, and crippled inside? Eh? What's it like?

A healthy swig of booze. Reels back. Looks to the sky.

PG Because I'm going be King of it all one day. You'll see. Because, look. There. In the big dome sky. Those vapours, there, melting shapes. It's me. Me riding whip-crack, and bareback in that chariot of fire. Surrounded by angels. Angels with wings of fireworks. Like. Oh. Like William Blake. Like Jack Kerouac. Like. Elvis. The bloody King himself. All bejewelled, and swivel-hip. And one day. That. There. That's going be me that is. Because this world is now ready to be chewed up, and spat back out. This world is ready steady fertile for all the new-born to breathe out a brave new universe. Because. I can hear it there. It's coming. It's stamping its foot, and splintering down the door. And there. Now. It's my name. On the lips and fingers of a million young things. All filled with colours on fire, ablaze with poetry. And music. And the holy buzz of electricity. Because we now. We are the new Gods. And we have come to kill the old Gods. And this now. This is our time.

PG holds the moment. The GUESTS from previous.

GUEST(F1) Look at the sky Ma. Look. It's me.

GUEST(F2) All them fluffy clouds. Don't they look really weird.

They run off, laughing.

PG Go on then. But you'll bloody well reckon. Eh? I'll show you all, I will. All of you!

Music crashes back in. PG staggers in. GUESTS notice. Present are BRIDEGROOM, and MATES (3).

PG Aye, aye, it is me. Evening all. I have arrived. How goes it?

PG has seen a BRIDESMAID.

PG What have we here? How do? What say you, bridesmaid, to a tipple?

B-MAID A what? What's that?

PG A Babycham? A quaff of gin?

B-MAID What you talking about?

PG What's your fancy?

B-MAID I wouldn't say no to a Snowball.

PG Wouldn't say no to a Snowball? Now that is my sort of lingo.

PG turns, and is met by BRIDEGROOM, and MATES(3). Stand-off. B-MAID disappears.

PG Ah.

MATE1 Look who it is.

MATE2 Peer Gynt.

MATE3 Peer fucking Gynt

BRIDEGROOM steps forward, nervous.

B-GROOM What do you want Gynt?

PG Hello Michael. Don't you look all grown up, and nicely turned out?

MATE1 Oi Gynt.

MATE2 He's taking the piss.

MATE3 He's taking the Michael.

PG Because I remember you. When was that? That time you had your first ever drink.

B-GROOM I don't think anyone wants to -

PG And you wet yourself.

B-GROOM What do you want Gynt?

PG And look at you now.

B-GROOM Eh? I'm asking you a question.

MATE1 He's asking you.

MATE2 Yea.

MATE1 He is.

MATE2 Yea.

MATE3 A question.

PG I merely came to say. Congratulations. Of course Cyn and me, we go back. Of course we spent many a night, whispering filthy nothings to each other. But so what eh? So what? That was then. And this, well. This is your wedding day mate.

PG smiles. They wait. Then it explodes. Everyone's shouting. B-GROOM in the middle of it.

MATE1 Let's do him.

MATE2 Have him.

MATE3 Dickhead.

PG Come on then. You bunch of sissy boys.

B-GROOM And, can I just say. I didn't wet myself. I spilt a drink.

MOTHER sweeps in. Everyone stops.

MOTHER Michael? Michael? Michael? Ah. There you are.

She notices PG.

MOTHER Well. Look who it is.

PG Hello Cynthia's mum.

MOTHER Peer Gynt.

MATE3 Wanker.

MOTHER And what, pray, are you doing here, Peer Gynt?

PG I just thought, you know. I'd, pop in.

MOTHER Pop in?

PG Yea.

MOTHER Look. Peer Gynt. I know you, and I know there is only one reason you would, pop in. So, what I'm going to say, is. Be a good boy. And.

She draws closer.

PG And what?

MOTHER Fuck off.

She turns to leave.

MOTHER Right Michael. Come with me. Now.

MOTHER exits.

MOTHER Now!

B-GROOM Yes Mother. What has occurred Mother? By the way, where's Cynthia?

She leaves. B-GROOM runs off after. MATES turns back to face PG.

PG Whoa lads. Alright. I'm on my way.

PG turns, and starts to leave. Then swiftly swings round, flicking the V's.

PG Yea. In your dreams. Arrivederci soft lads.

He runs off. MATES are slow-footed to respond. Band member steps to mic.

BAND.M. Settle down. We've got a special guest singer now. No, not Alma Cogan mate. All the way from the end of our street. Give up a warm hand. Sylvie!

SYLVIE steps out. Shy. PG appears, and watches on. She leans in to the microphone.

SYLVIE I've never done this before.

She starts to sing. A tentative, heart-felt version of 'Don't Treat Me Like A Child' by Helen Shapiro. An atmospheric echo to it. PG draws closer. As the song progresses they see each other. Electric. Song finishes. They stay looking at each other. Then scene shifts.

FATHER is knocking furiously on a bathroom door. MOTHER and BRIDEGROOM are there.

FATHER Do you hear me now? Cynthia! Come out this instant.

CYNTHIA No! Go away!

B-GROOM But why? I don't understand. Why has she locked herself in the toilet?

MOTHER How many times? It is not a toilet. It is a lavatory.

B-GROOM Cynthia? It's me. Why are you doing this?

FATHER She's gone mad. Like your Uncle Frank when he started eating all the soap.

CYNTHIA Go away. I hate you. I don't want to be married.

MOTHER Hey! You. You spoilt little hussy. You're married now. And that means, you have to just shut your cakehole, and get on with it for the next fifty years.

FATHER Well said Mother.

MOTHER Thank you Father.

B-GROOM Right. Stand back.

FATHER What are you doing now?

B-GROOM Cynthia! I'm coming in!

B-GROOM takes quite the run-up, and launches himself at the door. Pathetic.

B-GROOM Ow!

MOTHER Right. There's only one way to get this sorted.

FATHER Mother? Where are you going?

MOTHER One word Father. One word. Sledgehammer.

MOTHER leaves.

FATHER Did she just say?

B-GROOM She did.

FATHER Stay here. Bloody hell. A sledgehammer? Oh dear God, on a flippin' pogo stick.

FATHER is off after her.

B-GROOM Cynthia? Please -

CYNTHIA I hate you!!

Scene shifts. MOTHER is being pursued by FATHER. PG observes this exchange.

FATHER Mother! Mother? Will you stop now. You can't be doing this.

MOTHER Desperate measures Father.

FATHER But think of the cost. I'll have to pay for all the damages.

MOTHER She's locked herself in the lavatory Father? On her wedding day.

FATHER Yes, but, a sledgehammer? Mother? Where are you going find a -

They have gone. Scene shifts. SYLVIE, dancing, very alive. PG enters. They see each other.

PG Look. It's you.

SYLVIE It is. It's me.

PG So? Sylvie? I liked your song, by the way. Sylvie.

SYLVIE Thank you.

They have started to circle each other.

SYLVIE So? Who are you then?

PG Who am I? You don't know who I am?

SYLVIE I might do. But. Peer Gynt? Do you?

PG is enjoying this.

PG Now that is a good question. I might just spend the rest of my life trying to figure it out.

SYLVIE And what sort of name is Peer Gynt anyway?

PG I know. It's ridiculous.

SYLVIE Sounds as if you should be in a play or -

PG I like you.

SYLVIE likes this.

SYLVIE Do you now?

PG I do.

Music kicks in.

PG Are you dancing?

SYLVIE Why? Are you asking?

PG Yea. I'm asking.

They dance. Ecstatic. Alive. Others join in. Music dies down.

PG I really like you.

SYLVIE I bet you say that to all the impressionables.

PG I might do. But this time.

SYLVIE What?

PG I mean it.

They draw close.

PG Apparently. The Bride has locked herself in the bathroom.

SYLVIE Has she now?

PG On her wedding day, and everything.

SYLVIE Maybe she's scared.

PG And what Sylvie? What are you scared of?

SYLVIE answers. Playful at first.

SYLVIE Well. First off. I'm scared of. Being scared. I'm scared of the dark. Of bad dreams. And false teeth. Of snakes. And worms. I'm scared of? Loneliness. Of not knowing what love is. I'm scared I'll come and go, and no one will notice. I am scared of. All of this. This life. This precious time that we've been given. I'm scared that at the end of it. I'll look back on it. And think. What have I done? Who am I?

PG is taken aback. But impressed.

PG Wow.

SYLVIE And what Peer Gynt? What are you scared of?

PG I'm not scared of anything me.

SYLVIE Are you not?

PG I've got a bullet-proof suit of armour. Do you want
  to see it?

*PG makes a move. Touches her face. Goes to kiss her. She
pulls away.*

SYLVIE I have to go.

PG Why?

SYLVIE My Father. He likes to know where I am.

PG Stay. I won't try anything on.

SYLVIE Won't you now?

PG No. I'll stand here, and I'll just, look at you.

They look at each other. Intense.

SYLVIE Well, you can look at me. But don't build me a
  pedestal.

PG I think it might be a bit too late for that.

They carry on looking at each other.

SYLVIE Goodbye Peer Gynt.

PG Goodbye Sylvie.

*They stay, eyes locked, looking at each other. Then, a
voice, from off, HELEN.*

HELEN Sylvie?

SYLVIE Look. I really do need to, to go, because -

PG I love you Sylvie.

SYLVIE turns back, trying to understand this.

SYLVIE What?

Even PG is shocked he's said this.

PG I do. Yea. I love you.

SYLVIE thinks. A number of contradictory emotions.

SYLVIE And do you say that? What you've just said. Do you say that to all the impressionables?

PG No.

She stares, unbelieving.

PG Yes. I have done. Now and then. But this time Sylvie -

SYLVIE What?

PG I mean it.

SYLVIE reels.

SYLVIE No. You can't just say that. You can't just come out with something like that. Because. Are you messing with me Peer Gynt?

PG No. I'm serious. I'm deadly serious. I mean it.

SYLVIE thinks. Suddenly distraught.

SYLVIE I have to go.

PG But Sylvie? Why are you being like this? You must have felt it just then. I know you did.

She turns back on him.

SYLVIE You think you're such the big I am don't you?

PG And what's wrong with that?

SYLVIE I love you, he says. As though it, just, it's, it's just something you say. Just trips off the tongue. So easy. So, as though, it doesn't mean anything.

PG But I just said didn't I?

SYLVIE Said what?

PG Said. This time. I mean it.

SYLVIE So what? It won't last. Nothing ever does.

PG Why are you saying that?

SYLVIE Well, Peer Gynt. I hate you. You disgust me. And I don't want to see you ever again, because -

PG Go on then. You do that Sylvie. You do one. Pure and innocent, my arse-crack. You're just a prick tease you, a tart, dressed up as a, a sweet as butter wouldn't melt, vestal, fucking, virgin.

SYLVIE, shocked, and upset, runs off.

PG Sylvie? Sylvie! No. I didn't mean it did I? I just. Opened my mouth, and it all came spilling, and spewing out. Because. Sometimes the Devil sets loose in me, and, I say stuff, and I can't, just, put a lid on it. Fuck.

She exits. He looks on. Shaken. Then. MOTHER, pursued by FATHER. She is carrying a sledgehammer.

FATHER Mother? Saints alive woman. Will you put that sledgehammer down?

MOTHER No Father. I won't. I am a Mother on a mission, and she is coming out of there, even if they have to lock me up, and throw away the key.

FATHER chases after her.

FATHER Oh, if it doesn't rain, it thunderstorms.

PG follows them. FATHER re-appears, and he now has possession of the sledgehammer. They are now at the toilet with CYNTHIA locked inside. PG looks on.

MOTHER Hey. That is my sledgehammer. Give it back.

FATHER No. This has gone far enough Mother. Sledgehammers are not the answer.

B-GROOM Why doesn't she love me anymore?

MOTHER What?

B-GROOM She said she didn't love me. She said it's all been a terrible mistake.

FATHER That's marriage lad. Get used to it.

B-GROOM But I thought we were going to live happily ever after.

PG considers.

PG Look at them, squabbling like a bunch of grown-up kids.

MA arrives. Out-of-breath.

MA Peer Gynt! You great big, bloody mischief maker? Where are you?

PG Oh. But why not?

PG exits. MA is in the now in the midst of the lavatory mayhem

FATHER Mother? Please.

MOTHER Leave off Father. What are you doing here?

MA Where is he?

FATHER Where's who?

MA Peer Gynt. Where is he?

FATHER Peer Gynt?

MA That's right. Fruit of my troubled loins. Where the flaming bloody catastrophe is he?

MOTHER Well. He was here, but -

MA I knew it.

FATHER He was here? You mean -

MOTHER But I told him to sling his hook, and fuck off.

FATHER Oh Mother, now, I do not believe it.

B-GROOM She did say that.

FATHER The F word? Again.

MA But did he?

FATHER Did he what?

MA Did he, you know? (*mouths*) off?

MOTHER Michael?

B-GROOM What?

FATHER Did he, you know, (*mouths*) off?

B-GROOM I don't know. I was with you.

MOTHER You don't know? Well who does know?

VERA runs on. Breathless.

VERA Oh my. Oh. Calamity.

FATHER What now?

VERA Disaster.

MOTHER What's happened?

VERA Ruination.

FATHER Look. Don't just stand there saying words.

VERA It's Cynthia!

MOTHER What about Cynthia?

VERA She's gone.

B-GROOM What? She's dead?

VERA No. She's gone. She's run off.

FATHER Run off? You mean -

VERA He climbed up the drainpipe.

MA I knew it. I knew he'd do something like this.

MOTHER What do you mean? Who -

MA Who do you think?

VERA Peer Gynt!

B-GROOM What?!

FATHER Christ all bloody nightmare.

MOTHER The horror. The horror.

VERA He shinnied up. Like a man, I must say, who knew exactly what he was he up to. And she leant out, and then, he, well, he whispered something. What it was, well, anyone's guess, but, I'll say this, it did the trick. Because, then, oh my, oh, before you could say, whatever it is you say at a time like that, she hitched up her wedding dress. And very un-ladylike it was I must say. But there they were, down that drainpipe like, you know what off a shovel. And then, there she is with a man, who isn't her husband, hand-in-hand, on her wedding day, and scampering off into the sunset. As if they were the two going on honeymoon. And I thought, well, I had better tell someone. And now I have. And that's it. The end.

Silence. Shock. MA disappears. The mob starts to assemble around them.

FATHER I'll kill him.

MOTHER No. I'll kill him.

FATHER Well, after you've killed him. I'll kill him.

B-GROOM I don't feel right.

MOTHER Let's hunt him down.

FATHER Well said Mother.

B-GROOM Why is everything spinning round?

MOTHER Hunt him down like a wild animal.

FATHER And break all his bones, one by one.

MOTHER Well said Father.

BRIDEGROOM faints.

FATHER What now? Why is he lying down, now, at a
moment like this?

MOTHER Michael?

BOTH Get up.

*Music crashes back in. The lynch mob strides off. Amid
this, a small bed appears. A seedy hotel somewhere. A
couple, under the covers, having noisy, frenetic sex. This is
PG and CYNTHIA.*

CYNTHIA Oh yes. Oh God. That is. Yes! Yes! Yes!

*Boisterous orgasm. They emerge. Daylight creeps into the
bedroom. PG sits up. Thinks.*

CYNTHIA Wow. That was. Oh my God. That was
spectacular.

PG's mood is changing.

CYNTHIA That was earth-shattering. My Earth is
shattered. Do you want a fag?

No answer.

CYNTHIA Hey?

PG What?

CYNTHIA Do you want a fag?

PG No thanks.

CYNTHIA Go on. That's what you do after sex. You
have a fag.

PG doesn't answer.

CYNTHIA Suit yourself.

*PG makes a decision, and gets out of bed. Sits on the end,
and thinks.*

CYNTHIA Oh. That was, wow, that was amazing. We've
been doing it all night. I mean. We haven't even
slept. How incredible is that. We started a riot, and

now we're outlaws, rebels, on the run. I feel as if.
Yea. We're at the very beginning of something.
Everything else in our lives was just leading up to
this moment, now. Wow.

PG doesn't respond.

CYNTHIA Shall we, yea, shall we go and do something?
Go for a walk? And watch the sun come up, and
look at the dirty old river. And then we can find a
greasy caff, and have a greasy egg sarnie? And I bet
they'll be a jukebox, and we can play our song.
What is our song?

PG doesn't answer.

CYNTHIA Oh well, we can talk about that. You're being
really quiet. What are you thinking?

PG No. Not that.

CYNTHIA What?

PG Not. What are you thinking?

CYNTHIA I was just, wondering, because you weren't
saying anything, and -

PG picks up her wedding dress, and holds it out.

PG Here.

CYNTHIA doesn't know what is going on.

CYNTHIA What?

PG Get dressed.

CYNTHIA Don't be daft.

He carries on holding it out to her.

CYNTHIA Are you kidding? Are you, yea, you're
messing about?

PG It was alright while it lasted, but -

CYNTHIA But what?

PG I was drunk. You were drunk. We was full of ourselves.

CYNTHIA But you said -

PG What? I said what?

CYNTHIA You said you loved me. You said it loads.

PG Well, I didn't mean it did I. And love? Eh? What's that when it's at home? It's just a la-de-dah word for getting your end away.

CYNTHIA I feel besmirched.

PG carries on holding out the dress.

CYNTHIA I feel sullied. I feel desecrated.

PG Yea, alright.

CYNTHIA You used me.

PG No Cynthia. No. You used me. And I used you. We all use each other. That's how this, being alive thing works.

CYNTHIA You bastard.

PG And I'll tell you this. Women? Men? We're all as bad as each other.

CYNTHIA No we're not.

She stares him out.

CYNTHIA Men are far worse.

CYNTHIA grabs her wedding dress, and starts to get dressed.

CYNTHIA Christ all bloody mighty. I don't believe this, now, this is what is actually happening. Me, here, with you, saying, and doing this. What a bloody cocking mess. It'd be funny, if it weren't so tragic. Because. What am I going do? My life is now. It's in ruins. For this. A night of, what, of sordid lust in a seedy bedroom. I hate myself. But I hate you even more.

CYNTHIA is now dressed.

PG You'll look back on this, and think, I'm glad I did that. You'll tell your Grandchildren all about this.

CYNTHIA Yea, but I won't have any Grandchildren will I? Not after I've drowned myself in the canal.

CYNTHIA goes to leave, but turns back.

CYNTHIA Do you know what? I hope they find you. And I hope they get hold of you, and they beat you. And they kick you. And they keep on doing it, and doing it, until you're within a hair's whisper of death. And then, you have to spend the rest of your life, the rest of your long, pathetic life, crippled, blind, and all alone. You become the loneliest man who ever lived. If that actually happened. I would love that.

She makes to leave.

PG Cynthia?

CYNTHIA What?

PG You don't have any money to pay for the room do you?

A rumble, then, a huge crack of thunder. The bedroom starts to disperse. Thunder. Lightning. Rain.

PG now stands, laughing, arms aloft. MA arrives. It is noisy.

PG Come on rain. Drown me in it all why don't you? Because, look, here I am. Peer Gynt. The biggest rapscallion bastard the world has ever seen.

MA Peer! What in God's name are you doing now?

PG Alright Ma. How's life?

MA There's no time for any of this now, lad. You need to get going, because. Do you hear me? You need to leave, because. They're almost here.

PG I'm enjoying myself Ma.

MA Have you gone stark raving lunatic?

PG I can't hear you.

MA They're coming to kill you boy.

PG soaks up the rain. The lynch mob, slow-motion.

PG Don't you just love the rain Ma? Eh? Don't it just make you feel so alive?

MA Well, you won't be alive much longer if you stay here spouting all this nonsense. Because. Peer Gynt! Please, will you just. For me. For your Mother. Will you disappear.

PG There's some things Ma. There are some things, you can't be hiding from.

MA For crying out loud. How many times do I have to say it? You have to go. Now.

Another huge ear-splitting crack of thunder. Lightning. MA runs off. The mob is there. Led by FATHER, MOTHER and BRIDEGROOM. PG faces up.

PG Come on then.

They attack. Music accompanies. It is ferocious. PG is beaten to a pulp. Everyone disperses. PG lies, bloodied, and thoroughly, thoroughly beaten.

The rain starts to recede. PG starts to sit up. Eerie light. Then. DOREEN and MAUREEN. Glammed up, but very wonky. In terms of the style of the following sequence we have now moved forward to 1966 or thereabouts.

DOREEN Ooh look who it is.

MAUREEN Yea. It's him.

DOREEN It's, ooh, what's his name?

MAUREEN Yea.

DOREEN What is your name?

PG Peer Gynt.

MAUREEN That's right.

DOREEN Funny old name that.

MAUREEN Quite a mouthful though innit?

DOREEN Yea. But we all love a good mouth full though, don't we? Eh? Eh?

MAUREEN Oh my God. What is she like? You mucky slag.

They laugh, uproariously. They start to lead him somewhere.

PG So? Who are you then?

MAUREEN Who are we?

DOREEN Is that what he said?

MAUREEN You cheeky so-and-so.

DOREEN Who are we?

MAUREEN Who are you, more like?

DOREEN Eh?

PG Because. Where is this?

DOREEN You what?

PG Where am I?

MAUREEN Where am I?

DOREEN Where is this?

MAUREEN I've heard better chat-up lines from dead people.

PG What?

DOREEN Although. Here's a thought. Maybe you are dead?

MAUREEN Because, being dead eh?

DOREEN Who knows what that's like?

MAUREEN I don't even want to think about.

DOREEN Gives me the right old willies.

More laughter.

MAUREEN Oh my Christ. What is she like? Filthy cow.

DOREEN We're only messing you about.

MAUREEN Should have seen your face.

DOREEN You're not dead are you.

MAUREEN 'Course not.

DOREEN Be a funny old afterlife wouldn't it?

MAUREEN If this is what being dead was like.

PG Look -

DOREEN Here. Do you fancy a drink Peer Gynt?

PG Alright. Yea.

MAUREEN I fancy something fancy.

DOREEN Yea. I'll have something, ooh, with a cherry on the top.

MAUREEN Hey. I thought you weren't that keen on cherries.

DOREEN No. You're right. Here, Peer Gynt, you can have my cherry if you want?

MAUREEN What is she like? You filthy bitch.

Laughing uproariously, they sweep into a ramshackle Cockney boozer full of oddness. Life, and mayhem. Everything is off-kilter, and out-of-tune. A huge cacophony of voices. A piano starts up. Someone is holding a pig. Everyone bursts into song. PG looks on. A pint of something truly disgusting is put in front of him.

GEEZERS There you go/ On the house/ Go on/ Down your gob-hole/ Oi, oi/ Down the bollocks/ Go on/ Go on son/ Go on.

All look at PG. He looks back at the expectant faces. Then at the disgusting slop.

PG Do you know what? I'm not, actually, not that thirsty at the moment.

GEEZER1 You what?

They burst into song again.

GEEZERS What did he say?/ Having a laugh aren't you?/ Go on/ On the house/ Go on/ Drink it/ Go on/ Fucking drink it/ Arseholes/ Drink it.

PG drinks it. Not nice. The piano starts up. A right old knees up. PG doesn't see him, but KING has appeared. Grotesque. Dangerous.

PG Right. Well. Thanks for that. But, the thing is. I do need to, start thinking about getting home. My old Ma, she's going be worried sick. Is this the way out is it?

PG turns. Immediately runs into KING.

KING And where, oh where, oh where? Do you think you're going?

PG looks at him.

KING Sit down.

PG Like I just said -

KING Sit down.

PG I really do need to be heading home.

KING Sit down.

A chair has been placed. Whispers of 'sit down' from GEEZERS.

KING On the chair. That chair. There. Do you see it? I want you to sit on it. Now. On it. Sit on it. Am I speaking English? Sit on it. Sit down. On it. On that chair. There it is. Can you see it? Sit on it. Now. Sit on it.

PG sits. Relief. Applause.

KING You think you're a right proper it boy don't you?

PG What?

KING You think you're the right bee's bollocks don't you?

PG The bee's what? What are you talking about?

KING You don't know what I'm talking about?

PG No.

KING No Sir.

PG Eh?

KING Shut it.

PG But -

KING Shut up.

PG The thing is -

KING Shut your gob.

PG What?

KING Button it. Tighten it. Alright. Keep it schtum. Do you comprehende? Eh? Do you follow? Eh? Do you? Eh? Get the gist? Eh? Do you? Eh? Eh?

KING is right in his face.

KING Right. Now I've got your attention.

PG Who are you?

GEEZERS react to this.

KING Who am I? Who the fuck am I? Is that what you're asking? Is that what you're postulating? Is that what you want to know? Is it? Eh? Tell him who I am.

GEEZER4 He's the King.

GEEZER1 He's the fucking King.

GEEZER3 He's the King!

PG What?

KING Fuck's sake you muppet. I am the King. I am me, numero uno. Top of the fucking pops. I am the biggest ugly mug nasty bastard you will be running into today, tomorrow, and right up until the middle of the next millennium. And therefore, ergo sum, I am one you need to be paying attention to. Is that, now, is that crystal enough for you?

KING leans in.

KING And don't you even think about sneaking off. Because if you do, I will slip your eye out of your socket, and I will slice it open, and I will eat it, right here. And then I'll wash it down with a pint, and a pickled egg. And I love pickled eggs.

GEEZERS enjoy this.

KING I've seen loads of your sort over the years. Swaggering about, thinking they're the next big thing. Oh, but you. You? You're a right tasty half morsel you are. Look at the state of you. You look like a right little hobo who's been dragged through a fucking cow shed. You need to get your act together sunshine. You need to smarten yourself up. Because look at me. Don't I look the business? Eh? Don't I look tasty?

Holds out his medallion. PG inspects.

KING 'Cause do you see that? That's proper gold that is. Proper twenty-four karimba that.

PG is very taken. KING pulls it away from him.

KING Which, it just so happens, leads me, nicely-nicely, on to the point in question. Because, this, now. This is your very lucky, lucky, fucking, lucky day boy. Because how would you like it, if I offered you a small, but significant, slice of my success? Eh? What would you say? What would be your response? What would be your come back on that then? Eh?

PG looks on, confused.

KING Yes or no?

PG Er?

KING Yay or nay? Nay or yay?

PG Do you mean -

KING You say yes, we welcome you with open arms. You become part of the family. What is ours, is yours. You say no. And. Well, what can I say? Things would be different.

PG looks around. Everyone leering at him, muttering.

PG That is. Actual gold?

KING What do you say? What's it to be? Out with it. Tick-tock. Time don't wait for no one.

PG Well. This is really, unexpected.

KING What do you say?

PG My life at the moment, it's. I could do with a bit of a change.

KING leans in. As do all the GEEZERS. Crowd in on PG. They want an answer.

PG Yes. I say. Yes!

KING He said yes.

Huge cheers from everyone. More mad sing-song knees-up nonsense. PG is in the middle of it.

PG I always knew I'd do alright.

KING Well said my son. Bring her in.

GREEN WOMAN is ushered in. A young, grotesque woman. PG'S jubilation is severely dented.

KING That's it. This way my darling precious little girl. There we go.

GREEN WOMAN stands before PG. Quite a sight. Teeth missing etc.

KING Ah, now. Don't she look nice?

PG looks on.

KING Go on then. Say hello. Not that you need any introductions.

PG What's going on?

KING Is something the matter?

PG Is she? Is she pregnant?

KING Is she, what? Is she pregnant? No. She's got a bad case of tonsillitis. Of course she's fucking pregnant.

GEEZERS enjoy this. GREEN WOMAN waves coquettishly at PG.

PG Sorry, but, I don't know what's happening.

KING You reap what you sow boy.

PG What? No. That's, not, no, that's not possible?

KING Not possible? Listen to him.

PG But it isn't. Because. I don't remember ever -

KING Look. I know. I do have a very, everso, thin sliver of sympathy for your predicament. 'Cause there you are. You and your throbbing prick. Full of all that lusty spillage. All that spermatozoa. Swimming about. All you want is a handy orifice to dump it in. It can be a right proper headache. I understand. I'm a bloke. But, the thing is Peer Gynt. The thing is. Actions have consequences. And this. This is the consequence.

GEEZERS love the filthiness of the speech.

KING Right then. Where is he? What's he called? The funny little geezer in the dog whatsit? The Vicar. That's it. Where's the Vicar?

Uneasy, but some GEEZERS answer.

GEEZER1 He's done a runner.

GEEZER2 Yea. With a choir boy.

KING Fuck's sake, not again. Alright. Here. You do it.

GEEZER/V What?

KING You do it. You be the Vicar.

GEEZER/V Yea alright.

GEEZER/V is pleased with this.

PG Hold on. What's happening now?

KING You stand over there. And you, my lovely little sweet and fragrant. You park yourself just here.

PG Can I just? I really need to ask a question.

GEEZER/V Here. I just had a thought. I ain't got a Bible.

KING Yea. Good point. Anyone got a Bible?

Another GEEZER holds aloft a pornographic magazine.

GEEZER3 I got this.

KING What's that?

GEEZER3 It's a jazz mag. Although it ain't got any jazz in it, if you know what I mean?

Big laughs. Lots of masturbatory gestures.

KING Alright. That'll do.

KING grabs magazine, and hands to GEEZER/VICAR.

PG Is this, all this, that's going on now. Is this a nightmare?

KING Right then. Let's get this show on the road.

PG Of course. I must be wide awake in the middle of my own nightmare.

KING Oi. You. Enough with the talking out loud. Are you alright my darling?

G/WOMAN Yes Daddy. I'm blissfully happy.

KING Do the music.

A very wonky version of the Bridal March. G/WOMAN is lead down the aisle.

KING Go on then. Get on with it.

GEEZER/V Right then. Er? We are gathered here today, to, er? To?

Looks at the magazine. Can't help himself.

GEEZER/V To have a wank.

Uproar from GEEZERS.

KING Oi. Oi! Shut it. I said. Oi! Shut up. You bunch of fucking peasants. Do it again. And this time. Shut up. Do it properly. Christ.

Decorum of sorts returns. KING mutters, under his breath.

GEEZER/V We are gathered here today, to, er? To, er?

KING Celebrate.

GEEZER/V To celebrate. The, er, the? Er?

KING The union.

GEEZER/V The union. Of, er? What's his name again?

KING Peer Gynt. Fuck's sake.

GEEZER/V Peer Gynt. With -

PG What about that bit where you ask if anyone's got any objections?

KING Shut it.

GEEZER/V The union of Peer Gynt –

PG This isn't happening. It's all in my head.

KING Oi. What have I just said? No talking out loud.

GEEZER/V With –

The moment is broken by a farty stomach rumble. It is coming from G/WOMAN. Everyone turns to look. Concern.

KING Everything alright my darling sweetheart loveliness?

G/WOMAN Yea. Sorry Father. It must have been something I ate. I'm alright.

KING Right then. Where we were?

PG Look. I know I said -

KING Shut it.

PG It's just all this. It just seems to happening really quickly.

KING Get on with it.

GEEZER/V We are gathered here today, to –

KING No, skip that bit. Go to the bit where you do the business.

GEEZER/V What? You mean -

KING I want them fucking married. Now. Do it!

GEEZER/V Alright. Do you, er? Er? What's his name again?

KING Peer Gynt! Crying out, fucking, loud!

GEEZER/V Do you, Peer Gynt, take Green Woman to be your, er, your lawful, er, wedded, whatsit, you know? Thing?

All eyes turn to PG.

KING Go on. Answer him. Say it.

PG builds up the courage to say it. Mutters of 'Say it' from the GEEZERS.

KING Say it.

The words start to form on PG's lips. Then. Another convulse from GREEN WOMAN. More farty noises.

G/WOMAN Ow! Oh no.

KING What is it? Sweetheart? What ails?

G/WOMAN Fuck. My waters have broken.

She convulses. Panic starts to break out.

GEEZER4 Oh that stinks.

GEEZER5 That's disgusting.

GREEN/W falls to the floor, writhing in agony, preparing to give birth.

KING Get down there.

PG What?

KING Do your husbandly duty. Go on.

PG is on his knees. GREEN WOMAN gives birth. Screams from everyone. PG holds aloft the baby. It has a tail. It wriggles in his hands. Noise continues. PG throws the baby in the air. Everything goes dark. The sound of fighter planes. A bomb explodes. The stage clears.

Very dim light. PG is stood, trying to figure out where he is. Eerie. He wildly looks about. A number of figures in black appear at the edges. Snatches of scratchy voices in the underworld.

PG Where am I?

One figure is more prominent than the others.

PG Hey. You. Where is this? Who are you? Answer me.

The figures move around. We catch glimpses. Scary.

PG Come on. Show yourself. I'll fight you. Whoever you are.

PG throws some punches.

PG You don't scare me. Come on.

Then, a very definite voice.

VOICE You need to go round Peer Gynt.

PG What?

VOICE You need to go round.

PG What? What does that mean? That doesn't make sense. Who the fuck are you?

VOICE I am nothing. I am without shape. I am void.

PG Don't you start with all that mumbo-jumbo. Think you can freak me out. I'm not having it. Do you hear me?

PG flails, wildly. Can't see anything in the darkness.

VOICE I am you Peer Gynt.

PG I've had enough of this.

All of PG's answers now come back as an echo.

VOICE I've had enough of this.

PG Oi.

VOICE Oi.

PG Show yourself.

VOICE Show yourself.

PG I am Peer Gynt. And I'm not scared of anything.

VOICE I am Peer Gynt. And I'm not scared of anything.

PG Stop it.

VOICE Stop it.

The voices and echo builds. Then suddenly the space is overwhelmed with noise. PG falls to his knees. Noise builds and builds. The figures move towards him. Then.

Darkness. Silence.

Dawn breaking. PG, huddled, the dregs of a bad dream. Lurches forward. He sees HELEN. We have returned to the morning after the wedding. 1961 or thereabouts.

HELEN I've found him. He's here.

SYLVIE enters. They look at each other.

PG It's you.

SYLVIE It's me.

They look at each other.

PG You came looking for me?

SYLVIE Yea. I did. And now. Now I'm here.

PG I'm sorry for all those things I said.

SYLVIE I don't know why I did. Because. I just wanted to tell you. You're a dreadful, selfish person Peer Gynt, who doesn't care about other people's feelings, and I hate you, and I just wanted to say that.

PG Forgive me? I'm sorry.

PG falls down, such are his injuries. SYLVIE runs over to him. Holds him.

HELEN What are you doing now?

SYLVIE That's my sister.

HELEN I'd say hello, but I can't be bothered.

SYLVIE indicates that they'd like to be left alone.

HELEN Alright. But don't be long.

HELEN retreats.

PG So? What do we do now?

They kiss.

HELEN(*off*) Sylvie?

SYLVIE moves away.

SYLVIE I'm sorry. I need to go.

PG Stay.

SYLVIE It's just, it's my Father. Because if he knew about this. I mean. He'd go mad. And when he goes mad, he goes really, proper scary. And he hates you. And I heard him say it. He said. If any daughter of mine went off with him. Meaning you. He said he'd kill her.

PG Well, I'd kill him.

SYLVIE No! Don't say that. You mustn't say that.

PG Well, I'll fight him then.

SYLVIE No. I don't want any fighting. That won't solve anything.

PG Let's run off then.

SYLVIE What?

PG Let's go now. Me and you. Why not? Just. Start again, somewhere else?

SYLVIE thinks, tempted. HELEN appears.

HELEN Look Sylvie. If we don't go soon -

SYLVIE Alright. Just. Please. Give me, one more minute.

HELEN retreats, seriously unimpressed.

PG Because. These are our lives Sylvie. Sod your Dad. Sod this whole bloody town. I hate it. And we can find, I don't know, somewhere, a cottage. Miles from anywhere. And, I'll, yea, I'll build it myself. If it means me and you, we can be together. I mean it. What do you say?

PG holds out his hand. SYLVIE thinks. Starts to move to take it. HELEN appears.

HELEN Sylvie?

SYLVIE What?

HELEN That's a minute. You said, give you a minute. And that is exactly a minute.

SYLVIE doesn't move.

HELEN Ok. Make your own bed, and lie in it, because -

SYLVIE Alright. Yes. I'm coming. Goodbye Peer Gynt.

They kiss again. She starts to leave.

PG No. Sylvie! Wait.

PG rips a button off his shirt.

PG Here? Take it. Remember me.

PG holds it out. SYLVIE moves forward, and grabs it off him. She leaves. HELEN hangs back.

HELEN You. Disappear. And don't come back.

HELEN leaves. PG shouts after.

PG Sylvie? Sylvie?

Desperate. Then resigned.

PG Remember me.

PG exits, as a voice starts up, from off-stage. Other voices start to join in. It is the end refrain from 'A Very Cellular Song' by The Incredible String Band.

'May the long-time sun shine upon you/ All love surround you/ And the pure light within you guide your way home'

A group of HIPPIES appear. Their voices intermingle as they travel on their way. All very smiley. Bucolic. It is now 1970 or thereabouts.

PG appears. He carries an axe. He approaches. They carry on singing.

PG Hey. Excuse me? Can you? Do you mind? Oi.

They misinterpret PG's gestures. They encourage him to come and join them.

PG No. I don't want to join in. Can you, can you leave. Because. I live here. I live just over there. Oi? I said.

PG makes himself heard this time.

PG Shut the fuck up!

Everyone reacts.

HIPPIE1 He's got an axe.

HIPPIE2 He's going chop us up.

PG I am not. I am not going to chop you up alright? Look. Me put axe down. Me not chop you up. Ok?

Things have calmed down, but all very wary.

HIPPIE Ok man. We get the vibe. We're going split. Split!

HIPPIE3 Wow what a bad-tempered dude

HIPPIE4 What a freak.

They start to leave. PG sees bongos.

PG Hey. Oi. You left your bongos.

HIPPIE returns to retrieve. Tentative. HIPPIE lingers.

HIPPIE So? This is your place yea?

PG Uh-huh.

HIPPIE Getting your shit together in the countryside?

PG That sort of thing.

HIPPIE Impressive, man. It's cool. Being out here. Nature. Soaking up all that ozone. Feeling the grass beneath your feet. The sun comes up. The sun goes down. Wow.

PG Look. You. Whoever you are. Let's get this straight. I am not one of you. You, and your new tribe. I am myself. I've never read Herman Hesse, I hate the smell of joss sticks, and I am definitely, never, going be chewing on a lentil anytime soon. Because. See this. I built all of this myself. Every beam, every roof tile, every bit of it. Just me. If I want something to eat. I hunt it, I kill it, and I build a fire. And I cook it. Here. In front of this house. This house that I built myself. Nobody else. Just me. Nobody else.

PG slams the axe into some wood.

HIPPIE Are you ok, man?

PG Yea, and I'll be a lot more ok, when you're not still here, asking dumb-shit questions.

HIPPIE It's just. You seem, maybe, a bit strung-out? A bit, lonely?

PG I want you to leave. Now. Hippie.

HIPPIE I get the message brother.

HIPPIE, with bongos, moves off.

HIPPIE We're all hippies, man. It's just some of us, we don't know it yet.

PG You need to leave. Now!

HIPPIE scarpers. PG is angry and defiant.

PG This is my life. The life I've built. I will not. Not let the bastards grind me down. I am not lonely.

SYLVIE enters. A noise. PG turns. They look at each other.

PG Is that really you?

SYLVIE It is. It's me.

They look at each other. PG is speechless.

SYLVIE Aren't you pleased to see me?

PG Are you real?

She takes his hand, and places it on her cheek.

SYLVIE There. Do I feel real? And does this. Does this feel real?

She kisses him.

SYLVIE And here it is. The house you said you would build. Look at it. It's ideal. It's idyllic. Here it is, and you've built it all by yourself. With your own hands, and toil. And I want to live in it.

They kiss again. They emerge.

PG But? I don't understand. I have written so many letters. And then. Nothing. And now?

SYLVIE I never saw any of your letters. Not one of them. Because my Father, as soon as they arrived, he destroyed them. But then. Just the other day. By chance. I found one. And I read it. I devoured it. I fed myself on your sweet, touching, tender words. And I realised. When you wrote to me, and you said -

PG What did I say?

SYLVIE These are our lives. These are our lives, and we need to live them as though they actually mean something.

PG But? Your Father?

SYLVIE I disowned him. I disowned all of them. Of course they tried to stop me. But I left them behind. Because they are the past. They are my family no more. And, you. You Peer Gynt. You are my family now.

PG is very moved.

PG I promise. Dear Sylvie. I promise I will look after you. For, as long as. As long as time exists. Everything that is mine. Is yours.

SYLVIE As long as time exists?

PG I know.

SYLVIE That, now, that is a long time.

They laugh at their romanticism.

PG Because Sylvie. These last few years. I have been searching for, some, sort of, of meaning. And when I arrived here. I thought I shall work, and work, and in doing so, I would begin to find an answer. To the, the mystery, the enigma of who I am. But the more I tried to do this, the more my desperation, and my loneliness, wouldn't leave me alone. And night after night, they would haunt me. The night whisperers. The ill-bred thoughts of despair. But now, I realise. It was all leading, to this. This moment now. Because, you. You Sylvie. You are my answer.

SYLVIE is very moved.

SYLVIE I don't know what to say.

PG You don't need to say anything. All you need to do is, go inside. And let's begin the rest of our lives together.

SYLVIE I will. I'll do that.

PG And I will go, and find some wood. And then we'll build a fire. And we'll sit by it, and we will dream of the future. Our future.

They both start to move off, entranced with each other.

SYLVIE Peer? Look.

PG What?

SYLVIE It's the button you gave me. I kept it all these years.

SYLVIE moves into the house. She sings a refrain of 'Don't Treat Me Like A Child.' As she does, GREEN WOMAN emerges. Older, more grotesque than before. Accompanied by a feral child. PG moves further off. Can sense something isn't right. He turns, and comes face-to-face.

PG What the hell? Where did you creep out from?

GREEN W And look at him. All loved up. Makes me want to puke my guts.

PG What is this?

GREEN W And don't make out, you don't know who I am Peer Gynt. 'Cause look at you. You ain't changed. You're still the same old selfish bastard you always were. Because what about your poor old Mum? Eh? When was the last time you gave her a thought. Especially now. Especially now when she needs you most.

PG Ma? Why do you say that? What -

GREEN W 'Cause she's not well is she. She's dying. And you're swanning about here, singing Helen, fucking, Shapiro.

PG Who are you?

GREEN W You destroyed me Peer Gynt.

PG I'll destroy you now if you don't -

GREEN W Such, sweet breathy nothings. Such, sweet, cheap charm. Oh yea. All them words. All them filthy, naughty mutterings. They all came tumbling out didn't they? As there I was, spread out, spread-eagled, you humping away on top of me. As you heaved your load. Oh yes. Yes. Fuck me yes. You hollered, as you dribbled into me. And we gave seed to new life.

PG What are you on about?

GREEN W Come on, Peer Gynt, think back.

PG Answer me you mad bitch. You haggard whore. Or I swear, I'll -

GREEN W Or you'll what?

PG I'll carve you up.

GREEN W removes the axe from him.

GREEN W Like I care. The life you dumped on me.

PG And still. You carry on. What life did I dump on you?

The feral BOY makes himself known.

BOY Oi Mum!

GREEN W What?

BOY When are we going?

GREEN W I told you to stay over there, until I said so.

They shout over each other.

BOY But what you been doing? I thought you were just going go, and put the shits up someone. That's what you said. And then you said we'd go. I want to go home.

GREEN W Look. I really, really do not need this now. Oi. Shut it. Shut up! Shut up!

He shuts up.

GREEN W But I suppose. Now you're here. Come over here, and say hello to your Dad.

BOY is suddenly confused, and scared.

PG What?

BOY Eh?

GREEN W Come over here. Now.

BOY No.

PG My son? How can he be my son?

GREEN W I thought I just gave you quite a graphic description.

PG No way.

GREEN W Oh yes. Yes way.

BOY I'm going home.

GREEN W No. Oi!

BOY I hate you.

GREEN W Oi! Don't you run off now. You little bloody sod. Oi.

BOY has run off.

GREEN W Well, he takes after his Dad I'll give him that.

PG Listen to me. I want you to go, and -

GREEN W No. You listen to me Peer Gynt. You can't threaten me. 'Cause I know how to make your life a misery. 'Cause you think. You and her. Here in your soft-tinted, bed of roses, you think, it's all going be happy ever after now, don't you? Well, think again. 'Cause you didn't reckon on me, did you? 'Cause, I'm going be that face leering in at the window. I'm going be that shadow standing over you in the night, sucking the dreams out of you, and shitting them out as nightmares. I am the rotten tooth fairy maggot in your heart's desire Peer Gynt. And I will make sure everything you love, and cherish, will grow sick, and die a nasty, horrible, smelly death. Now. What do you think of that?

PG is shaken. SYLVIE enters.

GREEN W I'll be seeing you now. Bye-bye lover boy.

GREEN W exits.

SYLVIE Peer?

PG Yes?

SYLVIE Where are you? Will you be long?

PG I just need to go a little bit further into the woods.

SYLVIE I thought you might have been home by now.

PG makes a decision.

PG The Devil take me, and will you never. Never forgive me.

PG leaves. SYLVIE looks out. Senses something is very wrong.

SYLVIE Peer?

Silence

SYLVIE Peer Gynt? Will you come home?

Silence. It grows darker.

SYLVIE When did it grow so dark?

SYLVIE, alone, scared. The scene shifts.

MA, in bed, in hospital. Looks very ill. RUBY, her friend, is there with her.

RUBY There, Ada. You rest now.

MA I'm sick and tired of waiting Ruby. Because even now, where is he? Even now, he doesn't even show his face.

Voices, outside. Arguing over each other.

NURSE I'm sorry, the visiting hours have been.

PG But I want to see my Ma. Let me through. I want to see my Ma.

NURSE And the Doctor is on his way, so please, can you, please the visiting hours have been.

PG and the NURSE have entered.

RUBY It's alright Nurse. He can stay.

NURSE weighs up the situation. She leaves.

RUBY I'll be just out here Ada.

She leaves. PG and MA are alone.

PG Hey Ma?

Awkward. MA turns away.

PG I'm sorry Ma. I know I haven't been about. And I know I've been a bad son. But I'm here now. Look. I'm here now.

MA turns back to stare at him. PG feels like a small boy.

PG How are you feeling?

MA Well, apart from the throbbing head, the fractured hip, the broken rib, the cataracts, the bedsores, the unbearable pain in my chest, the water filling up me lungs, and the fact that I'm using a potty. I'm grand. Oh aye. Never felt worse.

Then serious.

MA I'm dying son.

Silence.

PG Would you like a cup of tea?

MA Would I like, a what? A cup of tea? That's rich, that is. What about a cup of tea anytime in the last ten years? That would have been nice. But now he just wanders in off the street, and he says, would I like a cup of tea? No. I don't want a cup of tea do I? When all I wanted all these years, was.

Stops before becoming too upset.

MA I nurture you. I bring you up. And I know I could have done a better job. But. I did do me best. And how do you pay me back? You just walk away, and don't say anything about where you might be, or what you might be doing. And I thought. So many nights. I sat there thinking. He's not coming back is he? Just like him. Eh? Just like the selfish so-and-so, I promised myself I wouldn't think about. Especially not when it came to this. And now I am thinking about him. And I hate myself for doing so.

MA is suddenly very scared.

MA Hold my hand. Eh Peer Gynt? Take my hand.

He takes her hand.

PG Eh Ma?

MA What?

PG Do you remember? When I was little. And for my birthday, you, yea? You gave me that car? That toy car? What was it? A dinky something. All shiny blue, and tin.

MA What about it?

PG I loved that car.

MA You did. I remember.

PG And you so hard up against all the time. And for you to buy that for me. I just. I just wanted to say thank you.

MA I'm sure you did.

PG No Ma. I didn't. I never did. But I'm saying it now.

MA fades away a little.

PG And, do you know what? I would have loved to have taken you out for a spin in that car.

MA Don't be daft.

PG Why not?

MA Because, well, it was just a toy car weren't it?

PG But just say right. Imagine. It was a real car. A proper car. Like proper people have.

MA That would have been nice.

PG So? Are you coming Ma?

MA Eh?

PG Are you coming for a spin?

MA What are you on about?

PG I'm pretending aren't I? I'm saying. Are you coming for a day out?

MA Oh. Go on then. Why not?

PG That's it Ma. You sit in the back. And I'll drive us.

MA But where are we going?

PG I'm not sure. But, eh, what about this? Let's get out the city.

MA That sounds nice.

PG And I'm starting her up now. Here we go. And, hey, how are the seats back there?

MA They're smashing.

PG I got the garage to shine up the leather, all buff, and smelling nice. What do you reckon?

MA I reckon it's proper fantastic. I feel like a Queen.

PG As you should Ma. Because I want this, now, to be one of them days you remember. I want this day to be one of them days, you never forget.

MA Well, it's already one of them.

PG And, look Ma. Look at all the fields. And the trees. So green. Green's a great colour. And all the bees. And the butterflies. And all those flowers. It's England Ma. Look at it. Don't it look beautiful?

MA looks. She is very moved.

MA It does.

PG And, oh yea, I forgot to say. We're going have a picnic. Because I've jam-packed a big old hamper full of all sorts. Sandwiches. And crisps. And apples. And, hey, marshmallows.

MA I love marshmallows.

PG I know you do Ma. And pop. Lots of pop. Because. Eh? You love your pop don't you?

MA Ah. You. You cheeky whippersnapper.

PG And we'll stop off in a bit. And we'll find a tree,
somewhere, in the middle of a big green field, and
we'll just sit there, and we'll take it all in Ma, and
soak up all that fresh air. How does that sound?

MA That sounds smashing.

PG Come on then. Let's see how this thing rattles. Let's
put a bit of breath in our sail now, shall we, eh?
And, feel that Ma. That feels good that does. The
breeze, and the wind in your hair, and the
sunshine, all warm and brilliant on your face. Are
you enjoying yourself Ma?

MA I am son. Thank you for a lovely day.

PG And now. Will you look at that? Right there, now,
right in front of us. It's one of them big, posh
country houses. Like, I don't know, you might see
in a film. Or, hey, in one of them books you always
used to read. With the dashing heroes, and the
heroines, and them always swooning, and being
swept off their feet.

MA is fading.

PG And look at it Ma. It's all white, and dazzling in the
sunshine. And, something must be going on.
Because, there's a few people standing about. And,
look. They've all started waving, and clapping.
Because. Hey. They've seen it's you that's turning
up. What do you reckon on that Ma? You must be
who they've been waiting for.

Music builds underneath.

PG So, eh, come on. Let's go see what all the fuss is
about. You take my arm, and. We're, now, we're
into the hallway Ma, and. Look up at that. That
chandelier, that's something that is, all sparkly,

with the light dancing off it. And now. Through some doors. And. It's the ballroom. Look at it. It looks like something out of a fairy tale. But it's not. It's you and me Ma. And there's hundreds of people, all dressed up smart, and fancy, in their suits, and their dresses. And, now, they're all turning about, and, they're all smiling, and. Listen to that Ma. They're all singing. And it's that song. That song you always loved. That one about Stardust. And now. I don't believe it. Making his way through the crowd. It's him. It's that fellar off the films you always used to talk about. Rudolph, what's his name? Valentino. He looks like a proper film star. I can see why you all fell in love with him. And he's. He's holding out his hand. And he's saying. Do you want to dance? Rudolf Valentino is asking you to dance Ma. And who could say no to that? Eh? Because, you. You, now, you do that. You get off. You enjoy yourself. You have a bloody good time. Because, you. Of all the people in this world Ma. You deserve it. Go on.

PG breaks. MA is dead.

PG Bye Ma.

Silence. RUBY enters.

RUBY Is she sleeping?

RUBY moves over to MA.

RUBY Oh. I say. Ada? Ada?

PG Look after her.

RUBY What? Why are you saying something like that, now, at a time like this?

PG I'm leaving. I need to get away.

RUBY Where to?

PG I guess, I'll find out when I get there.

PG stands. Music. PG2 (middle-aged) enters. They swap places. 'Identity' by X-Ray Spex kicks in. Televisions with static appear. He has a remote in his hand. Holds it up.

The loud sound of static. Black-out.

INTERVAL

ACT TWO

A low rumble. Builds. Then. A number of televisions burst into life. Information and noise overload. News footage. Crass game shows. Everything in-between. Fuzzy. Loud. Then they proclaim DUBAI.

A table strewn with the remnants of a very expensive, very lavish meal. Subservient WAITERS. A very hot and humid night. It is now 1982 or thereabouts. PG is the host. He is now a hugely successful, self-satisfied businessman of some sort. He has been holding a dinner party for four new potential business partners. These are RONNIE (American), BOB (Australian), FREDERIK (South African), and GUSTAV (German). Everyone is well-fed, and disinhibited with drink. They are toasting PG for hosting the dinner. They are the GUESTS. Their reactions have space for ad-libs/verbal underscore.

RONNIE Here's to Peer Gynt!

BOB Peer Gynt!

FRED I've had some meals in my time.

RONNIE But Jeez.

GUSTAV That was fucking wunderbar.

Noises of appreciation. Bang the table. Raucous.

PG Thank you my friends. Thank you.

GUSTAV Mein gut is about to go fart off really big.

PG Your pleasure, is my pleasure.

Laughter. Drink. Raucous.

PG More drink. We need more drink. Fill these empty
   glasses. Now. Not yesterday. Do it. Come on.

The WAITERS run about filling glasses. The GUESTS are very rude to them.

PG And here, now. Here is to opportunity.

RONNIE To opportunity.

GUSTAV Knock-knock?

BOB Who's there?

EVERYONE Opportunity!

PG And here's to the individual.

BOB Because, of course.

EVERYONE We are all individuals!

Much laughter. More drinking. WAITERS scurry about.

PG Now this. This my good, dear, wonderful friends. This is the life.

BOB leads with the first line. 'Is this the real life?' And then the others join in. 'Is this just fantasy?' PG launches back with 'I'm just a poor boy/Nobody loves me'. Then all the others chorus back with 'He's just a poor boy from his poor family/ Spare him his life from this monstrosity.' Very drunk.

PG But let me say this. I am a poor boy no longer. I am very, very, very, very, very, very rich boy.

They all join in on the very's. Money on the table is thrown in the air.

PG More. Now. Give these men whatever they want. Because whatever they want -

GUESTS They get!

Everyone drinks. Toast him again, as they do so.

RONNIE So? Peer Gynt? I have a question.

PG Ask away.

RONNIE Well, we were all wondering. What's the story? How the hell did Peer Gynt, I mean, Christ, how did he end up here?

BOB Yea. Spill the beans chief.

GUSTAV We have ways of making you talk Gynt.

PG What is there to say?

FRED What is there to say, he says?

PG I was born. I became myself. And I made a small success along the way.

RONNIE Jeez. Listen to the guy.

FRED A small success? After a meal like this.

GUSTAV What's the big mystery story Peer Gynt? Who are you?

PG Look. We've all made money have we not? Yes?

BOB I'll drink to that.

GUSTAV I love fucking money.

PG And we all know sometimes that. Yes? It pays not to ask too many questions. I'm not asking you questions Gentlemen. Am I? So all I'm saying is. Take me for what I am.

BOB Ok. Here's to not asking too many questions.

RONNIE Questions just lead to problems.

GUSTAV Wise fucking words.

PG But. I will say this. One piece of hard-earned advice. Never, ever, never get married.

RONNIE Hey. Now he tells us!

FRED Bit late for that my good friend.

GUSTAV I'd better not tell the wife. Eh? She'll want a fucking divorce!

Laughter.

PG Oh, but, be wary friends. The female urge to tie the knot, to surrender to the domestic. Resist. It saps the will. It dilutes the desire to discover the self. Because this. The impulse to make something of one's self. This is the over-riding credo that makes us all what we are. Rational selfishness. This is the be-all, the end-all. To create wealth. To create happiness. And this idea, this notion, that you must hitch yourself to one other human being. And then to live like this. Forever on, and on, until death do us part. All this does is build a, a cage to stop that that very purpose.

FRED Hey. Are you one of them intellectuals we hear about Peer Gynt?

PG This is my belief. As well as making money, I have spent many hours with my books.

BOB Brave words my man.

GUSTAV Big, fucking, brave words. I applaud you Peer Gynt.

RONNIE We all applaud you.

They applaud. Chant his name. PG feigns modesty.

PG Thank you. Thank you dear, friends. Colleagues. But now. The time is ripe. The time is now. And I wish to say to you. Let us make our dreams, our reality.

PG indicates. A very impressive architectural model of a supremely luxurious hotel complex appears. Music accompanies. GUESTS are open-mouthed at what is wheeled out before them.

PG And here it is friends. Gaze on, and revel, in wonder.

RONNIE What the hell?

BOB Christ!

FRED What is this?

GUSTAV Fuck me it's big.

PG Because this, now. This, fellow investors. This is a
hotel complex, the like of which has never before
been dreamt of.

PG presses his remote. An advert plays out on the screens.
PG fronts it, with very cheesy graphics and images.

PG This is luxury, and opulence fit for the late
twentieth century. Because, are we talking five
stars? No. Six stars? Oh no. This is seven stars of
the very ultimate in human lifestyle experience.
And it is to be built. Here. In this vast, parched,
desolate desert wasteland of blood, sweat, and heat.

PG sells them his dream.

PG Two hundred and eighty-eight rooms. All built with
the taste and refinement of what money desires,
money makes happen. Because, dare you dream. To
live. To exist like this. Like human deities stepped
down from your own personal helicopter. And
anything, and everything you wish to own, or
consume, will be here. Within this cathedral of
limitless luxury. This is the zenith of individualism
we have always imagined would one day be
possible. And then. When the day is done. You will
make your way, and you will fall into deep, blissful
slumber. And then. As it always does, in this
paradise on Earth. It will all begin, all over again.
Because you, dear Guest. You are one of the
beautiful people. You are one of the new Gods, and
we are here to serve you, because you. You deserve
this.

PG, using the remote, stops the advert. A moment, and
then a great response.

RONNIE Jeez.

GUSTAV My jaw has dropped so far down my fucking
face I don't know where it is.

PG So? Gentlemen? How do you like the future?

RONNIE Like it?

FRED He says.

BOB Like it?

GUSTAV We absolutely fucking love it!

Raucous appreciation.

PG But one more thing. One, more, thing.

PG holds the moment.

RONNIE What now?

PG The name.

A number of flashing signs. They proclaim GYNT LAND.

PG Gynt Land.

They are open-mouthed. PG waits for a response. Eventually.

BOB What?

FRED Gynt Land?

PG Yes.

BOB What the hell?

RONNIE Is this some sort of joke?

GUSTAV Are you piss-taking Peer Gynt?

PG No. Why would I joke about something like this?

GUSTAV It's just, like, your big fucking name, flashing away, all the time? Like this?

PG It is not a joke.

They consider.

RONNIE Ok. Let's go back a bit on this.

FRED We need to discuss this.

PG I've just explained. I've just given you the dream of how it's going to be.

RONNIE Yea. We all got that Peer.

BOB Gynt Land?

PG And what is wrong with Gynt Land?

GUSTAV It's a bit over the fucking top is what is wrong with it?

PG But, this is all my idea, my vision.

FRED Yea, but still -

PG But still, what?

RONNIE We're not saying we don't like it.

GUSTAV I don't like it. It's fucking crazy.

BOB Gustav!

GUSTAV Come on. Gynt Land? What the hell? It's really, really fucking deluded.

FRED I'm with Gustav.

PG Deluded? Crazy? Is that all you can say, after everything I've -

RONNIE No Peer.

PG Is this what you think?

No one answers back straight away.

PG You think I'm crazy? Just because I have dreams beyond the ordinary. That I'm, what? What did you say? I'm deluded? Is that what you think?

No answer from anyone.

PG And now, look at you, you just stand there, saying nothing.

BOB Hey. What about if we sit down, and we talk this through? I'm sure -

PG No. Meeting over.

RONNIE Hey now, come on.

PG The exit is over there Gentlemen.

BOB Peer!

PG You're just like all the others aren't you? All my life -

RONNIE What others?

BOB What are you talking about Peer?

PG Just because I said. And I will -

RONNIE What the hell are you going on about?

PG One day. I will be an Emperor. And a King.

FRED What?

GUSTAV An Emperor?

RONNIE Are you ok Peer?

FRED A King? Is that what he said?

GUSTAV I knew it. He's a fucking nut-case.

PG Get out! Now! You are no longer welcome. I wish you to leave. Now!

PG stares at them. He presses the remote control. A burst of television static. Then. An almighty explosion. The WAITERS don balaclavas, and pick up guns. Something akin to a terrorist attack. PG is manhandled, and placed on the floor. A gun is being held to PG's head.

PG What the hell? Look. I'm just a business man doing my job. It's those bastards. I bet they're behind this. Do you want money? I have money. I have lots of money. Or I did have. I think I may have just lost it all.

BALAC. Shut up, or I will kill you.

Gun being held to his temple. Then. PG takes out the remote control. A burst of television static. PG rises from the chair, and starts to run. Then. PG is running away from something. The sound of gunfire. Planes. AFGHANISTAN.

PG Yes! I'm free. I just, I just, need to find somewhere, somewhere to hide.

Crouches down. Some monkeys appear and start throwing rubbish/dirt at him. INDIA.

PG Get off. Where did you come from? Stop it. Don't you know who I am? I am Peer Gynt. Stop that.

PG takes out his remote. Static. Then. A burst of canned laughter. PG looks mystified. Remote. Static. Then. Static. PG is now in the middle of a game of cards. The stakes are high. Intense atmosphere. A small pool of light. MEXICO.

PLAYER I raise you.

PG And I raise you.

Money pushed in. The pile is high in the middle of the table.

PLAYER Ok. Let's see what you've got.

PLAYER presents his hand. Murmurs of appreciation.

PG Very impressive signor. But. I think, maybe?

PG presents his hand. Everyone is taken aback. Lots of shouting. PG starts raking in the money. PG takes out the remote control. A burst of television static. Then. PG is in the middle of the street being mugged. Someone is holding a knife towards him. Someone else is holding him. NEW YORK.

MUGGER1 Give us all your money.

PG Please. I'm just a traveller. I don't have much.

MUGGER2 Hey. What's this?

A wallet full of money.

PG That's all I've got.

MUGGER1 You lied to us man.

MUGGER2 We don't like liars.

They throw him to the ground. Kick him. Police sirens in background. Grow louder. MUGGERS run off. People are passing by as he crawls on his hands and knees. People rush past.

PG   Please Sir? Madam? Do you think, you might be able to spare me some cash? A few dimes? Please. Help me! Anyone? I just need a break. Come on. Oh God.

PG has a thought.

PG Of course.

Kneels, and starts to pray.

PG Dear God. Are you there? Are you listening? Because. I know I haven't given you enough thought in my life, and generally, I've been dismissive, but. I could really, really do with a helping hand. Look. I'm broke. And I'm desperate. I need a sign.

As he implores to God, a wealthy couple have entered, and they see him praying.

PASSERS-BY Hey look at that poor guy/ Give him some money/ There you go man/ Let that start you on the journey back brother.

PG Thank you. Yes. It will. Thank you.

PASSERS-BY Don't thank us/ Thank God.

PG I will. I'll thank God.

PG picks up the money. He has a thought. Looks skywards.

PG I'll thank God. Yes. I will thank the Lord!

Music builds underneath. PG breaks out in a big smile.
Laughs. He takes out the remote control. A burst of
television static.

The scene shifts to Las Vegas. A fat ELVIS leads in with a
version of 'Praise You'. The stage starts to fill up with a
number of very excitable Americans. The song builds. A
COMPERE steps out. Everything he says is underscored by
responses from the crowd.

COMPERE Oh my. Oh my goodness alive with the spirit
of the Lord who walks amongst us today, and
forever, and evermore, praise be, Hallelujah. Oh
my. How beautiful it is to see you all here today,
ready and willing, to be touched by the hand, and
the heart of the Messiah, the Saviour, the Holy
Father, the Lord God Almighty himself.

Hysteria is building.

COMPERE And now the moment is here dear brethren.
The moment for which we are gathered here in the
light and presence of the true Faith. The Power and
the Mercy. He walks amongst us. Here he is. Ladies
and Gentlemen. Peer Gynt.

Entrance music. ELVIS sings. The crowd goes wild. On
strides PG. Dressed in a white suit. He also wears a wig of
remarkable thickness. American accent.

PG Thank you. Thank you. The Lord is Great. The Lord
is in the building. Say yes. Say yes. He can't hear
you. Say yes.

The crowd join in.

PG Say yes to the Lord. Say yes to Jesus. Because Jesus
loves you. The Lord loves you. He cares for all of
us. He cares for all of us, even if we think we don't
deserve it. Even if we think our lives are small and

insignificant, and not worth the paper they're written on, he does care for us. He loves us. Say yes to Jesus. Raise the roof. Let him hear you good, and proud, and loud.

PG launches into full 'speaking in tongues' gobbledygook. Stops as suddenly as he began. Talks directly to a camera.

PG Now. A special message. I am speaking to all of you bearing witness back there in the sanctuary of your own living rooms. Jesus loves you. The Almighty God the Father who reigns in Heaven above us, and all around us, forever and ever, on and on, through never-ending eternal eternity. He loves you. And through me. His special presence here on Earth. He has given divine blessing to this holy fruit-based fizzy drink.

A can of fruit-based juice appears on the screens. It is called JESUS JUICE.

PG And he has also granted that it only be available, exclusively, through my own personal shopping channel. All you have to do is the phone the number. There, now. There it is. On the bottom of your screens. Phone that number, and make a financial donation, and this holy fruit-based fizzy drink will be, exclusively yours. Hallelujah. Praise the Lord.

More 'speaking in tongues' gobbledygook. Back to the audience.

PG Now. Let me come amongst you. Bless you brothers and sisters. I am without shame. I love the Lord. Do you love the Lord? We all love the Lord Almighty. Praise be. Now. Oh my. What do I see before me?

PG has alighted upon a very nervous looking woman in a neck brace.

PG I see a poor, unfortunate. I see a distressed, and broken soul in need of repair. Please. Come this way, and allow the mystery of the Lord to work his mysterious Power. Praise the Lord. What's your name sweetheart?

ELIZABETH It's Elizabeth.

PG That's a beautiful name. Now. I can't help but notice, but something tells me. Are you in a great deal of pain Elizabeth?

ELIZABETH I am.

PG Share your suffering with us Elizabeth.

ELIZABETH I had a very serious car accident. And the Doctor, he, he said -

PG And what did he say Elizabeth?

ELIZABETH He said. I was to wear this neck brace at all times. Because. If I didn't. Well. I might cause terrible damage to my neck for the rest of my life.

PG Take it off.

ELIZABETH looks shocked.

PG The Lord says. He's telling me now. I can hear him loud and clear. Take off the neck brace Elizabeth. That's what he's saying. Remove. And you shall be free.

Scared.

PG Do you believe in the power of God, and the Holy Spirit, and the mystery of Jesus, to heal and repair? Say yes Elizabeth. The Lord has spoken. Do as he says. Do as he says. Do it now. For him.

Quite insistent now. She, nervously, removes the neck brace. PG moves behind her.

PG How does it feel Elizabeth?

ELIZABETH Sort of tingly.

PG Sort of tingly? Now that's the Lord working his magic. Now move that neck for me Elizabeth.

ELIZABETH, very tentatively, starts to move her neck. Obviously in some discomfort.

PG That's it Elizabeth. A little bit more. Come on. Feel the power of the Almighty. He's here, and he's asking you to believe. Do you believe Elizabeth? Do you believe in the power of the Lord God Above in Heaven Praise his Glory to Behold?

ELIZABETH I believe!

PG Hallelujah!

PG grabs her by the head, and starts to twist and turn her neck. With force. ELIZABETH screams out in pain, as he does so.

PG Now. Elizabeth? Tell us all gathered here today. How does that feel? And how does that feel? And how does that feel?

ELIZABETH falls to the floor. Writhing. She is dragged away.

PG Yes. Praise the Lord himself. For he shall move in ever mysterious ways his wonder to behold. Oh my. Feel the Lord. Feel the Spirit of the Lord fill you up. Say yes to God. Wonder and amazement. We are in the presence.

ELVIS starts to sing 'I Believe in Miracles'. PG leaves WOMAN squirming on the floor. The noise and hysteria rises. A man on crutches has now been picked out of the audience.

PG Do you believe? Do you believe in the Power and the Glory? Do you believe in the Supreme majesty of the Kingdom of God?

CRUTCHES I do.

PG God can't hear you.

CRUTCHES I do!

PG So, throw them away. The power of the Lord be with you, and ditch those crutches.

The crutches are ditched. The man totters.

PG Walk for me. That's it. Walk!

PG commands, and the man starts to walk up and down.

PG And now dance. Move those hips. Dance for the Lord.

Caught up with the hysteria, he starts to dance. Ridiculous. PG lays his hands on. A violent reaction. The man falls to the floor. Someone in a wheelchair appears. Noise.

PG Do you believe?

W-CHAIR I do!

PG Do you believe with every fibre and organ in your Earthly body?

W-CHAIR I do!

PG Out of the chair. Now. I say. Rise from your chair. Rise from your chair!

They rise from the chair. One step, and then PG pushes them to the floor. More 'speaking in tongues'. PG moves and holds forth. A shift to PG in a spotlight. All hysteria/ noise stops.

PG Hallelujah. The Spirit of the Divine is alive and well, and spreads his wings, and blesses us with his Holy presence here today. Once more God has proved beyond all doubt that He is everywhere, and he is all-knowing, and all-seeing, and all-powerful. God is great.

The stage disperses, as a hotel room starts to assemble itself around him.

PG God is love. God is the truth, and the shining light in the darkness. God is the eternal flame of forgiveness and mystery. God is the universe. God is the stairway to Heaven. God is great balls of fire. God is the yellow brick road. God is the Wizard of Oz. God is winning the jackpot. God is Las Vegas.

The scene has now shifted to a hotel room in downtown Las Vegas. PG is with a hooker called DIVINE. She is hoovering up a fat line of cocaine. They riff back and forth. PG is very dishevelled. The light of a television.

PG God is Elvis.

DIVINE God is hamburgers.

PG God is Coca-Cola .

DIVINE God is cocaine.

PG God is feeling groovy.

DIVINE God is feeling horny.

PG God is dog spelt backwards.

DIVINE God is a pussycat.

PG God is pussy.

DIVINE God is the Devil.

PG loves this. She gyrates for him. PG is entranced by her.

PG What did you say your name was again?

DIVINE Divine.

PG Oh my.

DIVINE Sweet as. And half as evil.

PG The irony.

DIVINE Or Angel. Or the Virgin Mary. Take your pick. You're paying. I'm just saying.

PG No. Divine. Because, that now, that is a beautiful name. You move me Divine.

DIVINE Sure. I bet you say that to all the impressionables.

PG Maybe? Maybe I do. But this time.

DIVINE hoovers up another line.

PG This time Divine, I mean it.

He laughs at this. She doesn't.

DIVINE So? What do you want me to do?

PG Dance. I want you to, move your beautiful, sexy, butt for me.

DIVINE, using the remote, puts some music on. Something very AOR. She dances for him. Sort of sexy, but awful as well. PG puts his hand inside his boxers and starts to masturbate. After a bit, he comes. DIVINE switches the music off.

PG Oh my. Women? Why are you so, damn, dirty. Why do you insist on making us feel all these filthy, evil things?

DIVINE I'm just being me baby.

PG is distraught. DIVINE hands him a tissue.

PG You have a special soul Divine.

DIVINE I don't think so. I ain't got no soul.

PG We've all got souls Divine. I have it on very good authority.

DIVINE goes back to the cocaine.

DIVINE I was with my Mother when she died. And I didn't see no soul fly out. Or float out. Or whatever it is they're supposed to do when such a thing happens. All I saw was an old lady who weren't an old lady, or anything anymore. The soul ain't nothing but a human idea of something that doesn't really exist.

PG has been listening.

PG Marry me Divine.

DIVINE Now that would definitely come under extras.

PG I mean it.

DIVINE And so do I.

PG Marry me.

PG grabs hold of DIVINE.

DIVINE Hey Mister, leave off.

PG I'm sorry Divine, but please, don't call me Mister. Call me Peer. My name is Peer Gynt.

DIVINE Now that is some weird name.

PG I know. It's ridiculous.

DIVINE Sounds like you should be in a play, or -

PG I love you.

DIVINE Do you now?

PG I do.

DIVINE Well, that's fine, but –

PG Marry me.

DIVINE Ok. Look. You wanna pretend to be newlyweds or something, ok? But -

PG No. I'm serious. You remind me of someone.

DIVINE Do I now?

PG Yes. You do.

She looks at him.

PG Let's go now. Let's go find one of them twenty-four hour drive-in chapels, and say, I do. We'll drive there, and we can be man and wife before breakfast. And then we can go, and find a coffee shop, and we can eat pancakes, and we can play a record. And that record, that can be our song.

DIVINE What are you talking about? This is crazy.

PG I want us to be honest with each other. I want truth. Because.

He whips off his wig. DIVINE laughs, uproariously. PG stops the accent.

PG I'm not who I say I am.

DIVINE What the fuck? This ain't right. This is messed up.

PG And I've always wanted to discover the true self Divine.

DIVINE What the hell are you talking about now?

PG But the trouble is, I have no idea who I am.

DIVINE Look. I ain't no psychiatrist. I'm just a part-time hooker from Pasadena Avenue.

PG Or what about? We go off, and find a small cabin in the deep forest somewhere, and live there, and, be free, and be happy, and turn our backs on all of this, this, greed, and avarice. What do you say?

DIVINE Look. I think I'm going make my way home Mister, because -

PG No. You have to stay. Please? Sylvie? You have to save me.

PG violently grabs hold of her. A struggle. She falls on the bed. She reacts.

DIVINE Hey. You leave off now. Damn you that hurt.

PG I'm sorry. Forgive me. I didn't mean to hold on so hard.

DIVINE You're a mad man. Jeez. Fuck.

PG I'm sorry.

PG is overwhelmed with tiredness. His voice grows smaller, and smaller.

PG I suddenly feel, very, er. I'll just. And then. We can plan for the future. What do you say Sylvie? I need you to save me. I'm falling. Falling into the darkness.

Falls asleep. Very undignified. DIVINE clears the room of any valuables and money.

DIVINE Oh look at you. You sad piece of pathetic man. And I've seen all sorts in my time, but oh you, you Peer Gynt, you're extra special, with all your talk, and all your lies. I don't think you even know any more what is a lie, and what isn't. I'd guess, your whole life you've been swimming in it.

She draws on his face in lipstick.

DIVINE God bless. And fuck you Peer Gynt.

She exits. A very loud burst of static. PG sits up. Very startled. Dark. The light of the television.

PG What the hell? Where is this?

Remembers.

PG Ah. Of course. She's gone. Stripped me out, and left nothing but disgrace. And did I really say I loved her? Christ I must be mad. And now. This. To pick up the pieces from this. How?

Thinks.

PG I know. I'll re-invent myself. I'll write a book. My life. In words. All written by me. A search for the self. By Peer Gynt. Yes.

Grabs a pen and paper. Waits for inspiration. Gives up.

PG I'll start tomorrow.

Picks up the remote. A blast of static. PG is transfixed. We catch audio snatches of what he is seeing.

PG But what the hell is this? It's me. Look. As a young know-it-all.

Remote. Static. Then.

PG And now.

Remote. Static. Then. Remote. Static. Then. MA saying 'Hold my hand son'.

PG Ma?

Remote. Static. Then. SYLVIE singing.

PG And. Sylvie. Sylvie?

We can hear SYLVIE singing.

PG No!

Remote. Static. Then. Repeats. Snatches of 'Gynt Land' and explosions. He crawls towards the television screen. Horror. The hotel room disperses. He is grabbed and frog-marched, then dumped to the floor. The sound of a lockdown. Noise. Chaos.

Silence. Shadows. Cavernous. PG throws questions into the space.

PG Where is this? Where am I?

No answer.

PG Anyone there? Anyone?

A wary, cautious figure (INMATE) appears in the shadows.

PG Hey. You there. Where I am? Where is this? No, don't. Don't run off.

The figure disappears. PG, fed up, rants to himself.

PG I am so, sick, sick of it all. Being pushed from here to there. As though I've got nothing, nothing whatsoever to do with it. This is no way to live a life.

PG notices a number of figures start to flit across the space. These are INMATES(5). Dressed institutional. But with their own touches. They stare at PG.

PG Ah. Someone. At last.

They start to back away, wary, frightened.

PG Hey. No. Don't back off. I need to know. Where is this? Where am I?

PG waits. They emerge back from the shadows. Stand staring at him.

PG That's it. Come on. I just need some answers.

INMATE has crept back on.

INMATE I am the beginning of the end, and the final bit of both time and space. I am essential to creation, but also, I'm the end of the human race. What am I?

INMATES respond to this intervention. Share lines out as appropriate.

INMATE1 Oh shut up.

INMATE2 Always with the riddles.

INMATE3 He's stupid.

INMATE5 Yea.

INMATE5 Don't listen to him.

PG turns back to the INMATES. INMATE encroaches.

PG Look. I want to know who is in charge. Because. Where is this? I think there's been a mistake. I don't think I should be here.

INMATE I am the beginning of the end, and the final bit of both time and space. I am essential to creation, but also, I'm the end of time and space. What am I?

The other INMATES have started to shout him down before he's finished.

INMATE1 Oi.

INMATE2 Shut up!

INMATE3 Blah, blah, blah.

INMATE4 No one's interested.

He shouts over them.

INMATE What am I?

PG What is he talking about?

INMATE3 Don't listen to him.

INMATE1 He's a crazy person.

INMATE5 Yea.

INMATE2 He's not right in the head.

INMATE I am the beginning of the end, and the final bit of time and space.

INMATES again shout over him.

INMATE1 We don't want to hear you.

INMATE3 Shut up!

INMATE4 Shut up!

INMATE I am essential to creation, but I am also the end of the human race.

INMATES (*together*) Shut up!

INMATE Answer. I'm the letter E.

Groans, and frustration. PG looks on.

INMATE Do you get it? I am the beginning of the end.

INMATE3 Yes.

INMATE4 We get it.

INMATE4 We all get it.

INMATE But you didn't get it did you? Because if you did, you would have said. Because the word end, it begins with the letter E.

INMATE1 Shut up!

INMATE2 We said didn't we?

INMATE5 Yea. We did.

INMATE3 We don't want to know.

INMATE The end of the human race. That's the same. It's the letter E.

All the INMATES bear down on him. They pull him to the ground. They beat him up. PG looks on.

PG What are you doing? Stop it. There's no time for this.

Eventually it stops. INMATE crawls, beaten.

PG Ok. So? I would really like it, if I could, would it be possible to speak to someone? Do you understand? I want to speak to the person in charge.

INMATE1 The what?

INMATE4 The who?

INMATE2 Why do you want to do that?

PG Because I don't think I should be here.

INMATE1 That's nothing to do with us.

PG I know. That's why I'm asking you. Who's in charge?

INMATE2 We're in charge.

PG What?

INMATE1 The man.

INAMTE2 The boss.

INMATE3 Whatever you call him.

INMATE4 He left.

INMATE5 Yea.

PG So? You mean? That means. You? You're in charge?

INMATE1 I suppose so.

PG But hold on. If you're in charge? That means. We can just leave?

INMATE1 What?

PG We don't have to be here. Yes? We can just. Go?

INMATE2 Oh no.

INMATE3 No, no, no.

INMATE4 We can't do that.

INMATE3 No, no, no.

INMATE4 We're locked in.

PG But surely? Where are the keys?

INMATE2 What keys?

PG The keys? To the door. To the outside world. To let us out?

INMATE3 Oh no. No.

INMATE4 No one said anything about any keys.

PG Christ. I don't believe this. This is madness.

They all laugh at this. PG has had enough.

PG Alright. Yes I get it. Shut up! Shut up! All of you!
And you.

*They shut up. PG paces up and down, thinking all this
through.*

PG Because. Now what? I need to think. There must be
something we can do. We need to find a way, to,
somehow, escape, to get out?

INMATE1 Here.

INMATE2 Peer Gynt.

INMATE4 Why don't you?

INMATE5 Yea.

INMATE4 Why don't you be in charge?

PG What?

INMATE3 You be in charge?

INMATE1 Why not?

INMATE5 Yea?

INMATE3 Why not?

PG No.

INMATE2 You'd like that.

INMATE3 You'd be good.

INAMTE2 Better than any of us.

PG is obviously thinking about it.

INMATE4 You could be like?

PG What?

INMATE4 Like one of them?

INMATE5 Yea.

INMATE1 What do you call them?

PG What are you talking about?

INMATE3 An Emperor.

INMATE5 Yea.

INMATE2 A King.

This lands. PG tries to dismiss the idea, whilst very tempted.

PG No.

INMATE1 And this can be your little Kingdom?

INMATE2 Why not?

INMATE4 It's what you've always wanted.

PG thinks. They wait.

PG Well. I, er. I have always said. Maybe? One day? Alright. Yes. I will. Yes. I will be your King. I will be your Emperor!

An explosion of cheering from everyone. Including INMATE.

INMATE1 Yes!

INMATE2 Peer Gynt said yes!

They burst into song. A musical theatre number that celebrates PG's elevation to King/Emperor. To the tune of 'Hall of The Mountain King' (Grieg).

Oh Peer Gynt/ You want to be/ The chosen one who rules o'er me/ Over land and over sea/ Your name said far and wide

Oh Peer Gynt/ So you are he/ The glorious golden deity/ A human God to set us free/ Come claim your righteous Crown

Oh Peer Gynt/ They all will see/ You're the one 'tis meant to be/ The name foretold in prophecy/ Shout out 'Hallelujah'

PG is held aloft. A paper crown on his head. During the song, an elderly man has shuffled on. He carries a plastic

bag stuffed full of papers. This is PG3. He looks on.
Nobody seems to notice him. The song reaches a finale
moment. PG proclaims.

PG At last. Look Ma. I'm a King.

PG2 notices PG3. His status evaporates. Silence.

PG Do I? Do I know you?

PG3 stares. Only PG2 can see him. The INMATES disperse.

PG Do I know you? Answer me. I'm an Emperor. And
when I say so, you, you have to do, as I say. Who
are you?

Music. They swap places. PG2 leaves. Then. The roar of an
aeroplane. Mixed in with this are the sounds of a modern
airport. PASSENGERS arrive with chairs and form the
seats of a plane around PG. PG sits. Clinging on to his bag.
STRANGE PASSENGER arrives. Sits next to PG.

STRANGE P Ah. Here we are. Just made it. Such a
dreadful old faff isn't it these days? Airports. All
that hoo-ha just on the off chance that someone's
going to blow you up. What a world eh? Anyway.
Here we go.

The roar of an engine. They settle back.

STRANGE P So? He says. Trying to break the ice.
Returning home are we?

PG What?

STRANGE P Eh? Back to where it all began? After all
these years living somewhere else? And then one
day, you woke up, and you thought. Why not?
Embark on that long, bittersweet journey home
sweet home?

PG How do you know that?

STRANGE P Do you fancy a drink? A small snifter? Or a
big one. On me.

PG I asked you a question. How do you know that?

STRANGE P How do I know what? Ah yes. Excusez moi. Could I avail. Two alcoholic beverages of the spiritual persuasion. Thank you.

PG How do you know I'm returning home?

STRANGE P Oh lucky guess. I guess.

The drinks arrive.

STRANGE P Thank you so much. Very benevolent. Here we go good Sir. Chocks ahoy.

Hands drink to PG.

PG Thank you. But -

STRANGE P Bottoms upwards.

The roar of the plane engine. Everyone stands and moves their seats into a new direction. This happens with every plane noise.

STRANGE P Another? I think so. Hello my lovely. Could we possibly repeat? Soon as. There's a good girl.

Turns back.

STRANGE P Now. What were we saying?

More engine noise. This time with turbulence. PASSENGERS react. PG looks worried. Unlike STRANGE P. He is seemingly enjoying the experience.

PG What now? What's happening now?

STRANGE P Just a bit of a swirl. Turbulence. That sort of thing.

PG But, surely, we're not going to crash?

STRANGE P Difficult to say really. Statistically, you would think we'd be alright. But obviously. Somebody's got to be unlucky sometime.

PG I'm not ready to die. Not yet.

STRANGE P It's quite the thought isn't it? Hurtling through the Earth's atmosphere, at what, several thousand miles per hour. In what, if you think about, is simply a large piece of metal. One can't help but feel extremely vulnerable. The fragility of existence. All that. Chin-chin.

Another bout of turbulence. More reaction from others. PG begins to grow alarmed.

STRANGE P I must say. It's beginning to get really quite interesting. I think just one more. Take the edge off.

More drinks arrive.

PG I don't want any more to drink.

STRANGE P Nonsense. Get it down you. Numb the pain.

The plane lurches again, more than before. Everyone screams. PG looks alarmed. STRANGE P stays calm.

STRANGE P I don't wish to alarm. But I think we might be plummeting.

PG What?

STRANGE P Personally, times like this, I just like to sit back, and enjoy the thrill.

PG Who on Earth? Who are you?

STRANGE P Oh, and now, look about. How touching.

PASSENGERS have started to make phone calls. We catch snippets of what they're saying.

PASSENGERS Darling, I just wanted to say/ I love you/ Can I speak to the children?/ I love you/ Well can you kiss them good-night from me/ I love you/ Goodbye darling

PG What now? Why are they -

STRANGE P Apparently, it's what you do at a moment like this.

PG Who the hell are you?

STRANGE P's mobile has started ringing.

STRANGE P And, oh my, as if on cue. Look-ee here. It's for you.

Holds it out to PG. PG takes it.

PG Hello?

A fuzz of interference. A voice emerges. SYLVIE. Small, and very far away.

PG Hello?

SYLVIE Peer Gynt?

PG Sylvie?

SYLVIE Is that you Peer Gynt?

PG Where are you?

SYLVIE I'm waiting for you Peer Gynt.

PG What did you say?

SYLVIE I'm still here, waiting for you. Even after all this time. Peer Gynt?

The interference overwhelms her voice.

PG Sylvie? You're disappearing. I can't hear you. Sylvie? Sylvie!?

She has gone. The interference increases. The voices of the other PASSENGERS grow louder. STRANGE P takes back the mobile.

STRANGE P If I could just. Thank you kindly, everso.

PG Who the Devil are you?

STRANGE P Ah, now. There's a thought.

The plane veers again. Everything builds. Turbulence. Voices.

STRANGE P Oh. And here we go. Cling on. See you on the other side. We just, must have another drink sometime.

Noise. Screams. Builds. The plane plummets. Black-out.

Silence.

The sombre, soft tinkle of a church organ. There is a coffin. A few MOURNERS are gathered. There is a VICAR. He is not good at this sort of thing.

VICAR So, we are here, gathered, today. To say a, fond, adieu, and bon voyage to, a man. For he was a man. And there he is.

Looks over at the coffin.

VICAR It's always odd to think, really, but. There he is. Dead.

Tries to gather his thoughts.

VICAR For, indeed. What is a man? And why are we here? These are questions. Big questions. As is. What is the purpose of our lives? Because. We are born. A tiny, human bundle of, possibility, and potential. It is all before us. Life. The dream that is existence. It is ours to, er, seize, by the, the scruff of the neck, and, do, yes, do something with it for goodness sake.

Thinks.

VICAR Although, I think it's fair to say. The man here. His life was, well. He didn't quite manage that.

He is struggling.

VICAR But what is wrong with that? I hear you say. Because, an average life is, is, to be, as surely, as, celebrated as, a, not, average life? For we are all the same in the eyes of God. Are we not? Of course we are.

PG enters at the back, and looks on.

VICAR And now, here he is. About to embark on his final journey. And what, we may ask, what awaits? Because it does. The shining throne of Heaven, with all its attendant benefits, is now. His to savour forever, and ever more. Goodbye brave foot soldier of this Parish. You were here. But now. You're not.

Mournful music. MOURNERS gather around PG. An old-style pub. Miserable. PG is sat clutching his bag of papers. A few plates of sandwiches, sausage rolls etc.

DRINKER1 Ah well.

DRINKER2 That's it.

DRINKER3 Until the next one.

DRINKER4 Rum old business.

BARMAID, collecting glasses, approaches PG.

BARMAID You finished, love?

PG Thank you.

BARMAID Do I know you?

PG No. I don't think so.

BARMAID I thought, maybe, you looked familiar?

PG No. I haven't been here for many, many years.

She starts to move away.

PG Although. I did used to come here. A long time ago now. And I was wondering. If anyone remembers someone called Peer Gynt? Because -

MOURNER What was that? Peer Gynt?

Everyone notices.

MOURNER Peer, fucking, Gynt? Oh yea. I remember him. Who else here remembers Peer, fucking, Gynt?

DRINKER1 Who's that?

DRINKER3 Peer Gynt?

DRINKER2 Oh yea, I remember him.

DRINKER4 Bit of a wild one weren't he?

DRINKER5 I shagged him once.

MOURNER She killed herself didn't she? Because of him.

PG Who did? Who killed themselves?

MOURNER Cynthia. She drowned herself. And all because of him. What he did to her. And I'll tell you now. If he walked in here today. I'd -

MOURNER swings a bottle.

MOURNER I'd get him on his hands and knees. And I'd gouge his eyes out.

Everyone reacts.

DRINKER1 Hey!

DRINKER2 Arthur!

DRINKER4 Arthur mate!

DRINKER3 Put that down.

DRINKER1 Don't do anything stupid now.

MOURNER backs off. PG looks on, shaken.

DRINKER1 I think you need to make yourself scarce.

PG stands to leave.

DRINKER2 Come on. Let's have a sing-song.

A mournful twisted version of 'Agadoo'. Pub disperses. PG exits.

Dark. Shadowy. Then, from the shadows, emerges a RAG&BONE MAN, plus ASSISTANT. With cart. Creepy. Chilling.

RAG&B Any old iron? Any old iron? Put a bit of backbone into it. Any old iron?

Moves towards PG.

RAG&B Evening squire. How do.

PG looks on.

RAG&B You look surprised to see us?

PG It's just. I haven't seen someone like you, since I was a young man. I thought you'd all died out.

RAG&B Oh no. No, no, not us. No. We're still going strong. Aren't we?

ASST Yea. Going strong. Still going strong.

PG I never realised.

RAG&B There's always business to be found.

ASST Always business.

They circle. PG starts to move off.

PG Right then, I, er.

RAG&B Whoa, now, eh, oi, oi, hold up. Hold up.

PG stops.

RAG&B Where, may I enquire, do you think you're going?

PG I need to find somewhere to stay.

RAG&B You can't just be sauntering off, just like that, who knows where, and whatsit.

PG No. I've just arrived, and it's late, so -

RAG&B You can come with us.

PG What?

PG Why don't you jump on? We're going your way.

ASST. Going your way.

PG No. I don't. No. I don't think so.

RAG&B Come on.

RAG&B indicates the cart.

PG Thank you. But no.

RAG&B Look, Peer Gynt, I don't think you've quite grasped the gravity of your situation. You. Are coming. With us.

PG What are you talking about?

RAG&B Your time is up mate.

PG And what does that mean?

RAG&B It means. This is it. This is the very end of the cul-de-sac. Next stop, ding-ding, oblivion.

ASST. Oblivion. Ding-ding. I like that.

RAG&B You're not unique Peer Gynt. We've all got to go sometime.

PG No. That's ridiculous.

RAG&B We really need to get going, so, if you wouldn't mind.

PG No. I need more time.

RAG&B MAN finds this very amusing.

RAG&B Now, if I had a pound for every time someone -

PG I haven't finished my book.

RAG&B Oh dear God. I've heard it all now. Well, you should learn to read quicker mate, because -

PG No. I mean. My book. The book I've been writing all these years. About my life. I've been trying to, somehow, make sense of it all. Of who I am. I've been sat in a room for the last twenty years. More. Writing every day, and. Where is it?

PG is suddenly in a huge panic.

PG I had it with me, just now. Where is it?

PG starts to leave.

RAG&B Oi, where do you think you're running off? You can't escape us Peer Gynt.

PG is back in the pub. BARMAID. Echoes of 'Agadoo'.

PG Excuse me?

BARMAID What?

PG When I was in here before. I left something behind.

BARMAID You mean that plastic bag?

PG Yes.

BARMAID With all those hundreds of pages in it?

PG Yes. Where is it?

BARMAID I threw it out. I chucked it out the back, with all the other rubbish.

PG is off. Rubbish bins. Picks one up, and starts to search through.

PG Oh, where is it? My book? Where is it?

He finds something. Taken aback.

PG But what? What is this? Surely not. It's the car Ma gave me. All those years ago. All blue and shiny tin. No.

Then finds something else.

PG And now. Surely. It can't be. But. It looks so like. The button I gave to Sylvie.

Examines it, but then throws it away.

PG No. This is crazy, make-believe. I need to find my
  book.

Searches. Desperate. He picks out an onion.

PG And now. What is this? An onion? All rancid,
  bruised, and brown.

Goes to discard it.

PG But wait. It reminds me of the time. I was travelling
  in India. When I sat at the foot of a guru. And he
  held aloft an onion. And he said. This is man. This
  is man, unpeel, and you shall see.

He starts to unpeel it.

PG The outside is all worn, and bad. That can go. And
  then the next, is, somewhat fresher, but, still it
  tastes. Bitter. And then underneath that. It feels
  fresher. More full of itself. Of course. This is what
  he meant. The onion is man because, these layers,
  they are us. As we move through life, we adopt new
  costumes, new skins. And now, one more. And then
  finally. Of course.

Recognises. Laughs.

PG Nothing. This is man. Look. Man, is nothing. Peer
  Gynt. Is. Nothing.

*His laughs merge with a reoccurrence of the voices form the
VOID. He doesn't know where they're coming form. They
echo back on him. Eerie. Weird.*

VOICES Here Peer Gynt/ You need to go round/ We're
  the snows of yesteryear/ You need to go round
  mate/ Round and round the garden/ Like a teddy
  boy

PG Stop this. Where are you? Come on. Show yourself.
  And I'll fight you. I'm Peer Gynt and I'm not scared
  of no one me.

The voices disappear. PG is flailing at thin air. RAG&B arrives.

RAG&B How do P.G. How goes it?

PG No. I am not. No. I am not going with you.

RAG&B I don't wish to piss on your chips mate.

ASST Piss on your chips.

RAG&B But it's a bit too late in the day to be exercising the old free will.

PG No!

They circle him.

RAG&B Come on. Hop on. It'll all be over before you know it.

PG But why now?

RAG&B We've all got to go sometime.

ASST Go sometime.

RAG&B It's like my old Mum used to say. Time's a bastard, and it never stops.

The figures start to move towards him. PG has an idea.

PG No. I refuse. I am not going with you.

RAG&B Oh dear oh dear. Mate. Look it's not as though as you've even got anyone who's willing to say anything good about you have you? Eh?

PG You mean if I could, just find someone to speak up for me. I might be able to -

Out of the shadows emerges, PG1, begging.

PG1 Spare any change mate?

PG3 No.

PG1 Come on. I'm desperate.

PG3 Well, so am I. There's a lot of it about.

PG1 Oh, go on then. Suit yourself.

PG3 I will.

PG3 turns, and walks away. PG1 shouts after him. Momentarily we hear PG1.

PG1 Yea, you do that. 'Cause after all. What else is there? Eh? What else is there?

PG3 stops, turns, and looks at PG1. PG1 is suddenly very wary.

PG3 What was that?

PG1 Eh?

PG3 Do I know you?

PG1 What?

PG3 Look. Here's some money. Take it.

PG3 puts some coins in PG1's cup. PG1 looks very suspicious.

PG1 Are you after something?

PG3 Look. All I want you to do, is, come with me now, and, say a few words. About how I've been kind to you.

PG1 I don't want anything to do with the bizzies.

PG3 No. It's not the police.

PG1 They beat me up last time.

PG3 I promise. It's not the Police. Here's, look, here's some more money.

PG1 I don't fucking need it alright. All I want is you to leave me alone.

PG3 Come on. Come with me.

PG3 tries to grab hold of him.

PG1 Hey, get the fuck off me. I don't care who you are, or how much fucking money you shell out.

PG3 But, this could be a turning point. For your life. It could help you get your life back on track.

PG1 My life's well off the tracks mate. Has been for years.

PG3 Don't say that.

PG1 I used to think, I used to imagine how things might have turned out.

PG3 But that's what I'm saying. It's not too late.

PG1 'Course it's too late. My life's shit mate, and I don't want to live it anymore.

PG1 pulls out a knife, and holds it to his own throat.

PG3 No!

PG1 slits his throat. PG3 catches him as he falls. RAG&B and ASST enter.

RAG&B Friend of the family was he?

PG doesn't answer.

RAG&B Sort it out.

ASST Yea. I'll do that. Sort it out. I'm good at that.

ASST puts him on to the cart. PG turns on RAG&BONE. Desperate.

PG Is this because I've sinned? Is that it? Because, I've sinned too much.

RAG&B Truth is Peer Gynt, you've been decidedly mediocre regards the sinning.

PG But surely. After everything I've done?

RAG&B Like what?

PG Like? Everything. The way, I've, I've followed my own selfishness?

RAG&B So-so.

PG All the lies I've told?

RAG&B I've seen a lot worse.

PG And then there's all my money. When I had money. Do you know how I made it?

RAG&B You've got a lot competition. Especially these days.

PG No.

RAG&B Oh yes. You, Peer Gynt, when it boils down to it. You, have been decidedly average in every which way you would like to think about it.

The body is on the cart.

ASST Times have moved on mate.

RAG&B We live in a Godless world now.

ASST He has ceased to be.

RAG&B He is an ex-God.

Starts to wheel off the cart. PG1 on board.

PG No. That's not true.

RAG&B See you at the crossroads Peer Gynt.

PG turns, and he is now in a burnt-out church. Desolate. PG shouts into the darkness. An echo.

PG Is there, anyone? Anyone there?

From the shadows, emerges an extremely decrepit PRIEST. Bad-tempered.

PRIEST Yes? What do you want?

PG Is this still a House of God?

PRIEST What can I say? His name is still on the deeds.
But I can't say, I've seen him about much recently.

*Suddenly the space is full of screeching bats. PG flails
helplessly. Scary. Then suddenly they are gone.*

PG What was that?

PRIEST Oh, it's bats. We have bats. Lots of bats.

PG You should do something.

PRIEST We don't have the money. And anyway, I like
them. They're company.

Silence.

PRIEST So? Is that it?

PG I need somewhere to stay.

PRIEST Not another one.

PG Because this is still a place of sanctuary? When I
was a child, I used to be dragged here every
Sunday. To sit and listen to endless words, and
sermons, about God. And how if we spoke to him
nicely. He would forgive us.

PRIEST That was a long time ago. We get three or four
on a Sunday. Sometimes, no one.

PRIEST exits. PG shouts after him.

PG There are people after me.

PG is a man alone.

PG Go on then. Shuffle off. You decrepit, senile, old
waste.

Silence. The sky is suddenly full of stars.

PG And now there. Look. The universe stretched out in
all its shapes and echoes of stars, both dead, and
alive. Above us only this. And it reminds me of
when, a young man, he stood, not far from here,

and he, oh, he was so full up of himself. And he looked up, and he revelled in the eternal strangeness, and mad mystery of it all. And he imagined, he dreamt, what his life might be.

PG looks out to us.

PG We come to light. We grow dim. And then. Darkness.

Silence. But then, sunrise. Beautiful.

PG And now. As if, to take the piss. Here it is. The everyday marvellous. The sunlight grows hard, and it breathes, and it comes rushing forward in all its colour, and all its complexity, and all its commonplace, astonishing, splendour. Look. It's the easiest thing in the world. To look.

PG looks.

PG Why do we not, every day, each and every single moment of our lives, why do we not drown ourselves in bliss, and wonder at the sheer, ridiculous, miracle of it all?

Then. SYLVIE, singing. PG sees her. At home, bathed in light. She still looks the same. Young, and beautiful.

PG Sylvie? Sylvie? It's me. It's Peer Gynt.

She doesn't hear him. RAG&B and ASST enter.

RAG&B And now the end is near.

ASST And so we face.

RAG&B The final curtain.

PG No, not now.

RAG&B No more of your prevarications Peer Gynt.

Puts his hand on his shoulder. PG reacts, violently.

PG No! Get off. Get off! I am not going with you.

RAG&BONE retreats. PG turns, and he stands before SYLVIE. She sees him.

PG Look. It's me.

SYLVIE Yes. It is. It's you.

They look at each other.

SYLVIE Well. I must say. This is a surprise.

PG Sylvie. I'm so. I don't want to say it, because it sounds so, trite. But I am. I'm sorry. And I have thought of you. Every day. You've been there, with me. In my imaginings, and my daydreams of what, of what might have been. And I know I should have done something. Been in touch. But, somehow, the time has never. I have always been too busy thinking of myself.

SYLVIE Would you like a cup of tea?

PG Thank you. That sounds. Splendid.

SYLVIE rises. She leaves, singing. Full of youthful energy. PG looks out.

PG I love your view.

PG is full of sadness.

PG From your window here. This street. As the day grows dark. When I was first born. When I first breathed life, I looked out on a view like this. Obviously there are more cars now. There is so much more of everything in the world. The world moves on. Everything moves on.

SYLVIE returns with tray, and tea. She is now, though, an old woman.

SYLVIE What was that?

PG sees her. Overwhelmed.

SYLVIE You said something. I'm sorry, I didn't hear it.

PG Here. Let me help you.

PG takes the tray, and rests it between them.

SYLVIE Thank you. Let it brew for a minute.

Silence.

PG So? You knit?

SYLVIE I do. But not so much these days. Not now my eyesight is not what it was. This is a scarf for one of my Grandchildren. I have seven Grandchildren.

PG And may I ask?

SYLVIE Three. Two boys. And a girl. They've all done well for themselves. One is in London, but the others are still close by. They visit. We speak on the phone. I feel very loved.

PG And is - ?

SYLVIE He passed away. Five years ago now. He was a good man. We were very happy.

She considers.

SYLVIE I didn't love him the way I loved you Peer Gynt. But I did love him. Very much. Because after you left me, there. In the woods. You had broken me. I had no one. And, he seemed. A good choice. That sounds maybe, dispassionate. I don't mean it to be. I've been very blessed.

PG speaks, very softly.

PG I'm sorry.

SYLVIE We were very young.

PG We were.

PG bursts out. Heart-rending.

PG Where have I been Sylvie? Where is Peer Gynt? After all this searching. Where am I?

PG kneels before her.

PG Please. Sylvie? Save me.

SYLVIE No. I'm sorry, I -

PG You must.

SYLVIE I can't do that.

PG You said just now. You loved me. You loved me more than anyone else.

SYLVIE I did. I do. But. It's too late. Far too late Peer Gynt.

Then. A knock on the door. It is RAG&BONE.

SYLVIE There's someone at the door.

Another knock. They both know who it is.

SYLVIE Shall we put the radio on?

PG Yes. Why not?

PG turns on the radio. Sad and beautiful. Another knock on the door.

SYLVIE I like to sit here. Sometimes all day. Listening to the radio. I find it a comfort. I think, maybe. A tiny bit louder?

PG turns up the volume. The sad and beautiful music fills the room. PG walks over to SYLVIE. He holds out his hand. She takes it. They hold each other close. The knocking, from everywhere, grows louder, and more insistent. The music also grows louder, and more stirring. They dance in the light. Darkness encroaches. The knocking continues. Even more insistent.

Black-out.

THE END

Printed in Poland
by Amazon Fulfillment
Poland Sp. z o.o., Wrocław

62454604R00065